Also by Rick Fordyce

Glen: a novel

On the Wide African Plain-and other stories of Africa
(forthcoming)

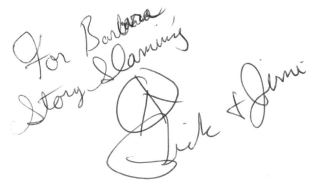

*For Barbara,
Story Slamming*
Rick & Jimi

I CLIMBED MT. RAINIER WITH JIMI HENDRIX'S HIGH SCHOOL COUNSELOR

And other stories of the Pacific Northwest

by

Rick Fordyce

I Climbed Mt. Rainier With Jimi Hendrix's High School Counselor
© 2014 Rick Fordyce

Back cover photo: Rick Fordyce. *Stan looks back into his pack.*
Interior design by Vladimir Verano, Third Place Press
Cover Design by Merrimack Media

ISBN: 978-1-939166-42-5
Library of Congress Control Number: 2014932397

A Merrimack Media Edition
www.merrimackmedia.com

For the Fab Four

Who taught me you could laugh all day, make passionate art,
then laugh again until you went to bed. Repeat the next day.

Contents

Contents ... continued

I Climbed Mt. Rainier With Jimi Hendrix's
High School Counselor

I CLIMBED MT. RAINIER
WITH JIMI HENDRIX'S
HIGH SCHOOL
COUNSELOR

Back then, the Fuhrer Finger had deep snow on it. It was a steep chute on Rainier's south face, rising above the Nisqually Glacier and ending at the Kautz Glacier, which rose up from the west flank.

Back then, in the spring of 1976, you could climb Mt. Rainier for thirty dollars. Or, more accurately, climb Rainier, Baker, Guy and Si, learn rock-climbing, glacier travel and crevasse rescue, and get home-made brownies after class. Except for clothing, thirty dollars, total, all equipment supplied.

That was the 'basic climbing class' the Cascade Alpine Club offered over its six weekend spring course. You overviewed at the headquarters in West Seattle and got brownies; conditioned on Mt. Si; rock climbed at Anacortes; climbed Guy Peak; glacier and crevasse trained on Rainier's Nisqually Glacier, and, when the weather broke, went up north and climbed Baker.

Actually, climbing Rainier wasn't officially part of the class, but unofficially it became so.

It was in the class that I met Stan. He was by far the oldest of us dozen or so students: late fifties, short, on the stocky side—but obviously in mountaineering shape—and with the friendliest, most approachable demeanor, easily the class's most likable participant. I believe, at twenty-four, I was the youngest; most everyone else being slightly older, with the exception of one of the instructors—there were five—who was closer to Stan's age.

As the class progressed we got to know one another a little more intimately, seeing as we were all spending six weekends together, at first just during the day, but later, while on the climbs, overnight. I was a student at the U dub, the only one still an undergrad. Some in the class were grad students, others, older, living and working in the community.

Stan, obviously, was one of those 'older and working in the community'. He was a high school counselor, he eventually told us. He worked at Garfield. He had been there a long time, he told us. He had been there since the mid-1950s, almost twenty-five years.

The weather system that had been forecast all week came on the first Mt. Baker attempt. Baker was supposed to be the course's final climb, the climax, the graduation. We had completed all the other curricula over the five previous weekends, including, under a cloudless sky, self-arrest, roped glacier-travel, and crevasse rescue, the previous weekend on Rainier's Nisqually Glacier. Because Baker was scheduled for June, a normally favorable weather month, and because we clung to enough hope that maybe the system would break, that maybe we could climb it after all, we trekked with all our gear up to the Nooksak Glacier, set up camp, and awaited the morning to see. But along with all the other climbing parties—we were now down to just eight students as four had dropped out over the course of the spring (but still with all five instructors)—we packed up and went back down in the steady fog, drizzle, and wind that had greeted the new dawn.

We made it the next weekend, though, the sky now cloudless—and now just seven students as another had dropped out—trudging to the summit, where, because of the howling wind, we stopped only long enough for a quick lunch and a few photos.

Along with the spectacular views—south to the Cascade volcanoes of Glacier, Rainier, Adams, and St. Helens; west to Puget Sound and the Olympics—and the wind on the summit, there were three other things I remember about the Mt. Baker climb. The first was the large number of "tourists", who, because of the warm June weather, had followed the roped climbing parties across the glaciers and up the snowfields in sneakers and blue jeans, experiencing, apparently, adrenal-fueled strength and Admiral Byrd-like ambition and confidence. They eventually all turned back before the summit, but a few actually made it to the top of the Coleman Headwall.

The second is of watching one of the tourists who had fallen, cartwheel uncontrollably down the headwall. To one side the steep chute resembled Everest's Hilary Steps, with a long line of roped climbing parties extending up from the bottom to where the route disappeared over the top, everyone now stopped in their tracks, watching, unable to do anything as the man cartwheeled past. Down he went, nothing in his hands, sneakers and mopped-hair end over end, like a stuntman in a movie, the stopped climbers stunned, none having paid attention beforehand to what was below the quarter-mile long chute, everyone assuming, considering how high up the mountain it was, that he would soon be airborne at the top of some precipice, and that we were witnessing the final moments of his life. But, in fact, to one side the lower chute flattened out; he stopped cartwheeling and now slid feet first, like a toboggan, rolling over a couple of times, before slowing and coming to a stop. With dozens of frozen-in-their-tracks climbers looking on—the line in the snow looking like the miners going up Yukon Pass in the old Klondike Gold Rush photo—this is what we saw: the man laid there for a moment, got up, brushed the snow off, looked once back up the headwall, then walked a few feet over to the trail and continued down.

I don't remember where Stan was on the Baker climb, which rope, but he was there, somewhere; like me, he wanted to be sure he got his thirty dollars worth. The third thing I remember about the Baker climb is that it was then we learned that Jimi Hendrix had been one of the students Stan had counseled at Garfield High School in the late-1950s.

It was also then, after we got back to the cars at the trailhead, that the instructors made the class an offer. They, the instructors, were planning to summit Rainier the first weekend in July, and any student who wanted to come could join them at no cost, all equipment supplied.

For whatever reasons, only two students took them up on the offer. Myself and Stan.

With dozens of previous Rainier summits between them, the five instructors—four men and one woman—decided they would attempt a new and more challenging route, one that none of them had tried before.

And that is how it was that we came to ascend the Fuhrer Finger.

In the early and mid 1950s, the value of higher education—even high school—did not have the near-obsessive sense of necessity that it (justifiably?) has now, Stan had told several of us on the high mountain slope during one of the earlier weekend classes, ice-axe in hand, face and arms slathered in sunscreen, smiling widely from behind cheap sunglasses. Before the post war baby-boom and the higher stakes of a strong formal education, it was much more common and much less stigmatizing to not complete public-school, he told us.

You've heard the stories: a grandparent or great-grand parent who completed only eighth grade—or sixth or fifth. Lived a long and happy life.

"I counseled him for a long time," Stan now said to just myself as we waited at the back of the rope in the pre-dawn darkness at the base of the Fuhrer Finger on the south flank of Mt. Rainier, the five instructors huddled in furious debate above, Stan and I at the bottom of the second rope, unable to hear the heated discussion.

"I first had him when he was a fourteen year-old freshman..." Stan went on, looking up at the huddled instructors, the bright beams of headlamps crisscrossing the steep snow field, Stan only half paying attention to what it was he was talking about, mostly, like me, wondering what the instructors were arguing about. "...He was a sweet kid, then, but..." We were moving again. The first rope, with three instructors, was continuing up the steepening chute. The second rope, with two instructors in front and me and Stan at the back, digging in and following, our crampons cutting into the fresh steps the first rope had just created, trudging upward, bright stars of the night still shining above, the faintest crease of light visible on the far eastern horizon. To each side were walls of dark rock with a nearly vertical carpet of snow above us.

Making their way to a secure point along the rock wall, the lead rope stopped once more, the instructors again huddling, arguing animatedly, Stan and I at their mercy, there in the middle of the Fuhrer Finger, not invited to join the discussion, and in a sense knowing why.

"Believe it or not," Stan said, continuing his tale, "I actually convinced him to drop out. Not exactly what you'd expect from a counselor." Below the beam of his headlamp, Stan gave a small smile, one conveying trust in the irony of what he had just said, and confidence, as well as a lack of concern with my reaction, with how a layman might take it.

With the light now increasing steadily to the east— we, along with the white cones of Adams, St. Helens, and Hood, about to catch the first rays of the rising sun— there on the near vertical chute of the Fuhrer Finger, the instructors arguing above us, I looked at Stan, nodded, and said: "Huh." As in: huh, that's interesting.

"Yeah, I thought it was the best thing for him at the time. Still do. It wasn't working out for him—school. He was all set to join the army. And he'd picked up the guitar by then. There were other places to learn."

"Huh," I said again.

With the frozen-flow of the Nisqually Glacier now spread below us, a tiny corner of Paradise and the parking lot to one side and the jagged peaks of the Tatoosh range across the valley, to Stan's confession that he had persuaded seventeen year-old Jimi Hendrix to drop out of high school, I once again said: "huh."

With the slight smile—the smile of 'I'm an old man now and I always tried to do what I thought was best and there's nothing that can be done about any of it now anyway, and I hope to live my final years enjoyably—Stan looked at me and shrugged his shoulders. Then he turned and looked at the great beacon of the sun as it rose above the eastern horizon, its rays beaming onto the tops of the Cascade range. "Wow, look at this," he said.

We forgot about Jimi after that, soon at the top of the Fuhrer Finger, and, eventually, at the summit of Mt. Rainier in the bright blue of the new day.

On top, the instructors informed Stan and me that we would not be going back down the Fuhrer Finger, that we would be descending via the standard Kautz Glacier route, that despite, collectively, their dozens of previous Rainier summits on a wide range of routes, they had never experienced such fear and uncertainty as what had just transpired on the Finger, that they had come within a hair—a guitar string?—of abandoning the climb, eventually voting three to two to continue.

"Thanks," I said to Stan when we were finally back at Paradise and the cars, our faces burned red from sun and wind, our bodies in a previously unknown physical state after having been pushed beyond a limit we had not known to exist.

"For what?" Stan asked.

"I don't know," I said. "For everything, I guess."

He smiled and waved good-bye, and we got into our cars and drove home.

A FIST FULL OF PEOPLE

The man who could pass for young set the heavy pack down on the side of the road and looked back down the highway to check on how well the cars could see him and thought they could see him pretty well and then stuck out his thumb and leaned away when the trucks roared by. One after another the Americans streaked past in their sleek colorful automobiles: mostly small ones; some big, some made to live in: rolling houses. And inside, the riders, sporting bright, middle-class summer clothes, and with seemingly clean, healthy heads of modernly cut hair, each looked out at the tall lone figure with the large pack standing on the side of the road. And never would a single car stop…except sometimes…

Harvey and Don

Harvey and Don picked me up on the side of the road in the early evening light, there in the forest along the river in the northeast corner of Washington, and as soon as I had thrown my pack into the backseat and jumped in, Harvey asked me how I liked his new one hundred dollar car. These were northwest good ol' boys, but Harvey was bad. Harvey was a bad, crazy bastard, and I mean crazy: drinking his beer and driving all over the road, but not at all drunk, just not into the task of driving, and telling me these crazy stories: Like the other week when he and a buddy picked up two chicks in a bar late one night and drove with them two hundred miles into Montana to visit a friend of Harvey's and after a while the girls started complaining and said they were tired and wanted to go home. And the next morning Harvey got left in this little town, and when he saw his buddy and the two girls driving off in the car—*leavin' me in some little town two hundred miles from home*—he just looked at 'em drivin' off and said—*fuck you, fuck you guys*. Then he had to hitchhike home.

And then another story about when Harvey got a job one time working down in this mine pit, and at first Harvey thinks that the other guys who were down there with him thought he was a narc. He's pretty sure they thought he was a narc because he had short hair, and Harvey was real scared at first because he figures anything could happen to you down in some mine pit if the other guys down there with you think you're a narc. *But shit*, Harvey said, laughing and drinking his beer and driving all over the road, *they didn't do anything to me.'*

Harvey and Don scared me a little; but they took me a long way and smoked some pot with me and offered me beer. But their talk was too crazy, like about guns, and how Harvey would always be ready if someone ever tried to jump him or something, and how he would never take a gun hitchhiking with him, but if he was sleeping out in some field or someplace, he' be sure that he was lying down so that he could see if someone was coming up on him with a gun or something.

Then it got uncomfortable when they dropped me off in a field along the river to sleep for the night with no one around after what they had been saying.

Tom, Dave, and Sue

Tom was in the small café at the edge of the mountain town, talking with the middle-aged waitress and eating a veal dinner with fries and drinking coffee, when I walked in asking if anyone knew of a good place in the area to camp that night. And Tom told me about a campground that was just out of town on the river and then said he'd show it to me and that he knew the area well because he worked for the Forest Service. Then Tom and the waitress, who were the only people in the café, except for the cook, told me to order up some food and Tom said he'd pay for it and I argued with him for a while but he ended up buying my dinner. Then he offered me his backyard to put my tent up in if I decided that I didn't like the campground but when he took me out to look at it I liked it a lot and so I stayed.

The next day Dave, who also worked for the Forest Service, came out to collect a five dollar a night camping fee and I told him about how Tom had brought me out and Dave said that if I were to tell him that I had just arrived that morning he wouldn't argue with me and then I'd just have to pay for one night, because we both thought that five dollars a night to camp was pretty high. Then he said he'd tell Sue, who would be coming out to collect the next morning, that I was out there and was all paid up.

The next morning Sue came out and I had decided to move on and on her way back into town she gave me a ride and I told her about how Tom had brought me out that first night and Sue, driving the small pickup on the forest road, her eyes watching the road, said, "yeah, they just don't come any friendlier or nicer than Tom Jacobs".

Dean

Hallelujah! how was I to know then that when Dean picked me up on the side of the road this morning he had been sent by *Him*, and that I could at long last, once and for all, be saved! Hallelujah! how was I to know that Dean's two seemingly innocent questions: "how do you feel about the present condition of the world", and, "how do you get two giraffe, a male *and* a female, to come out of evolution when it's hard enough to just get one?" (?!?) How was I to know then that these were *His* questions to me and would lead to two and one half hours of *His* message, through Dean, as we rolled through the forest covered mountains of northern Idaho in Dean's, battered, 1978, Datsun pickup. And how was I to know then that when Dean let me off on the side of the road, forty miles into Montana, *His* word, soothing and true, would now be mine to take throughout life's long, suffering, praisethe-lord, hallelujah!, last. Godamighty I think I been saved!

Pete

Pete, in his late forties, was there at the campground on the mountain lake in the north Montana woods with his wife and their good sized trailer and one morning he walked past my camp and asked how I was doing. Then he told me about some places to see in Whitefish and Glacier because that's where I told him I was headed.

The next day, in the early evening, at the edge of the clear mountain lake with the low mountains, forest covered, rising up fast from the lake's edge, Pete was there sitting at a picnic table, watching the lake, then, when it was best to watch it, and I came up from my camp to watch it too and I saw Pete and went over and asked him how he was doing. And when he answered he sounded a little drunk and he acted a little drunk; but it was hard to tell for sure and I didn't get close enough to smell his breath, and I wasn't going to ask him; but he looked glad to see me and then he told me about some things. He told me about how he had graduated from West Point, like his father, and then been one of the first to go to Vietnam in the early sixties, and that he had been real gung ho then.

"God damn were we ever gung ho, then," Pete said, looking hard at me. "Sixteen months that first tour," and then looking at the lake, "but it was just no damn good, no damn good for anybody. Now," and looking back, "if I had a kid who was going to get drafted now, I'd send him to Canada. And there'd be no hard feelings about doing that. I did the military route, and I got something out of it, but now I see it's no way for anyone to go. I got something out of it, but later it got bad. Six months back in the states and I was back down there for a second tour, and it was the worst thing I ever saw. That second tour they had me in charge of nothing but niggers, and one night, I'll never forget it, twenty of 'em I had under me on a river boat, they had me in charge of this river boat, and one night it was bad. They sent us to clear mines out of the river, forty miles out of Saigon, and the shelling was going on everywhere real bad that night, and when I'd try to get those blacks to do something they just wouldn't: 'Why?' they'd ask me, 'Why are we here? What have we got to gain?' Now I can't blame 'em. I don't have anything against blacks, but when they get together and start talking amongst themselves, they won't do anything for anybody. Then after that second tour I quit.I quit because of her," and Pete pointed at the quiet trailer sitting at his campsite back in the trees; and I thought of the woman inside.

"You can't blame her," I said.

"No, I guess not," Pete said. "She said that if I went back there again, I was getting all ready for a third tour, she'd divorce me. So I quit."

Then a breeze came in off the lake and Pete's round face looked up from the table perched on the bank above the lake where he was sitting, and at me who standing there opposite him; and the wrinkles on his face deepened and his eyes looked old and tired and pleading, and then became serene, and looking far into my eyes and pointing again at the trailer, he said, "I quit because of her. Because she said she'd divorce me." Then he looked back at the lake. "No, the military is no good. That's one thing I know for sure now."

And it was almost dark and I told him that I had to get back to my camp and get a fire started and I went back and got one going.

A BAD PLACE

Mitchell Gray came in from the cool mountain-morning to the old lodge-like restaurant and sat at a table in the light of the corner windows. He was the first customer of the gray spring day, and through a door near the back he could see the waitress and several other employees talking and moving quickly about in preparation for the large Sunday crowds that would come later. Over a stereo, an old Rolling Stones song played loudly, filling with rock music the rustic, high-ceilinged restaurant at the center of the small town out the Mt. Baker highway in the interior of the North Cascade Mountains.

Now ready for a customer, the young pleasant-looking waitress came out the back to Mitchell's table. "Would you like coffee?" she asked with a smile, showing a full mouth of straight, white teeth.

"Yes, and cream, please."

She returned a moment later with a menu and a glass cup filled with coffee and two small half-and-half cream dispensers. The blond-haired waitress with the sharp features smiled pleasantly again at the three-day, camping-worn Mitchell sitting in the dull light of the tall windows.

"Will it get very crowded later?" Mitchell asked, opening one of the cream dispensers.

"Oh, yeah, they'll be here. But I'd guess by the size of the crowd in the bar at closing last night that right now they're all still sleeping."

Mitchell gave a short laugh and looked out the window. He hadn't slept well last night alone in the tent, the loud pattering of raindrops hitting the tent fly, awakening him, the racing of thoughts in his mind keeping him awake. Outside, the gray marine clouds came in low up the valley, covering the tops of the steep mountains down to a few hundred feet above the green valley floor. Mitchell looked again at the menu. "I'll have the pancakes with the egg."

"How would you like the egg?"

"Over medium."

She was very pleasant looking.

Smiling again, the waitress finished writing down the order and took the menu and went off to the back of the restaurant. Outside in the damp air, the clouds continued to come in low up the valley. It was the end of May and everywhere there was new green: the moss-covered trees on the valley floor, full; the thick forest going up the mountain sides deep in greens: the firs and cedars, dark; the maples and cottonwoods, light; all glistening in rain-drenched dampness.

Taking a sip of the coffee, now brownish in color from the cream, Mitch spread before him the front page of the large Sunday newspaper and began to quickly skim the bold type of the headlines. As his thoughts began slowly to drift to the headline-events, they suddenly returned to the room when, from behind, there came the voice of a man speaking to Mitch over the loud volume of the music: "Is that the Bellingham paper, there?"

Out of the corner of his eye, Mitch saw a sandy-haired man wearing blue-denim jeans and jacket come up from behind and bend over the table, straining to see the name of the paper. He spoke again, quickly and in jerks: "Would you mind—if for just maybe a second—I could take a quick look—at the movie page?"

Turning around, Mitch said: "No, go ahead." And he pushed the paper down the thick, wood table to the tall young man who now sat down at the end of the bench. Finding the section he wanted, he opened it full in front of him.

"Okay—yeah—here we go. I was planning on going into town today." He glanced up at Mitch. "I was going to take my girlfriend to a movie—but it's gotta be an early one—'cause I gotta be back here by five to work."

Mitch took another sip of coffee and looked again at the man. He thought that he didn't look like one of the people who would work at a place like this, this far up in the mountains. It was mostly college kids from the university down in Bellingham who were the help. He looked too old to be a college student to Mitch. And although he had said girlfriend, Mitch saw that he was wearing what looked to be a wedding band on his left hand where it is understood that they are placed. But he didn't look to Mitch like someone who would be married, either. He didn't seem to have that kind of reserved aura of responsibility and conformity. There was too much of a boyish state about him, although Mitch could see now that he must have been in his early thirties.

"Damn. Nope. Can't do it," the boyish-looking man said. "Nope. Nothing until 4:30. Damn. Oh, well."

"You live up here?" Mitch asked.

"Yeah, I was living down in Bellingham, but I got a job up here in this place, so now I'm living up here." He looked again at the stack of newspapers in front of Mitch. "What's going on in the playoffs? Lakers win?" Setting the arts page back on the pile, he found the sports section and opened it in front of him. Mitch still had the front page. "Yeah—all right!" the boyish-looking man blurted, "kicked ass." He turned the page and glanced again at Mitch. "You going back down to Bellingham today?"

"All the way back to Seattle, eventually," Mitch said.

"Seattle? No shit?—whoa." The boyish-looking man gave a kind of grin as he looked at another page of the sports section. "Man—that's a bad place. I'm from Seattle."

Steve got out of the car in the dark drizzle in front of the small Wallingford house and walked up to the front door and knocked. He kept his left hand in his front pant pocket where the ninety dollars was and glanced back down the quiet residential street toward the traffic light at the intersection. Bollick opened the door of his mother's house and let young Steve in and led him down to his room in the basement. There was a large checkered quilt hanging on one of the walls and an old stereo on the floor below the quilt and beside the stereo a large box of records. One of the records spun on the turntable.

"You'll like this stuff a lot," said Bollick, skinny in his jeans and flannel shirt, hair spilling over his ears and collar, as he pulled a cigar box out from under his bed and took out a few small plastic bags, each filled with several, finger-thick patties of a dark, soft-looking substance.

"Yeah, good looking shit," Steve nodded, holding one of the bags up to the light. He opened it and breathed deeply, the strong odor of the hashish filling his nostrils. "Looks like Afghani."

Bollick took a metal pipe from his pocket and, breaking off a small piece of the block, placed it into the bowl and handed the pipe to Steve. Striking a match, he reached over and held the flame above the bowl. Steve sucked deeply on the stem and the tiny chunk caught flame and glowed red. Keeping the match lit, Bollick took the pipe from Steve and held the flame to the bowl, inhaling deeply on the stem as the smoking chunk glowed bright then turned white and went out. Sitting on the well-worn couch in Bollick's dimly-lit room, Steve tapped his foot to the music and took out a cigarette and glanced around. Things were beginning to move. "Yeah—yeah—this is pretty good stuff, all right." He dug into his pocket and handed the money to Bollick.

Bollick struck another match and held it out for Steve's cigarette. "Yeah, it's been keeping me high all week… What are you doing?"

"Taking a picture."

"Why?"

"I don't know…I just got this. They're kind of cool."

Bollick shook his head, he dropped the match in the ashtray and reached over and turned up the stereo. "Hey, you going to Dwight's party Friday?"

"Hmmm, yeah, it's this Friday isn't it? Yeah, I'll probably be by." Steve put the camera back in his pocket, he took another drag from the cigarette and moved to the edge of the couch. *"Well, hey, I gotta get going. I'll see ya around,"* and he stood up and walked to the door.

Driving on the street again through the dark drizzle, Steve looked at the bright headlights coming toward him and the long lines of red taillights leading off in the distance in front. I hope Mom and Dad aren't up, he thought behind the wheel, bent toward the windscreen. Oh well, I'll just go in the back door. And he drove on faster down the dark wet street.

Mitch lowered the newspaper and looked again at the young man sitting at the table across from him. "Really? What part of Seattle are you from?"

"North end," said the sandy-haired man. "I grew up around Wedgwood."

"Is that right? I grew up around Lake City. Oh, my name's Mitch. You know, you almost look familiar."

"I'm Steve…" he held his hand out to Mitch, "…Peele."

Mitch set his coffee down and shook the boyish-looking man's hand. "Peele. Yeah. Yeah, I think I recognize the name. But you know, there was actually somebody else who I thought maybe you were; did you know Michelson?"

"Michelson? Yeah—Dan?"

"Actually I thought maybe you were his older brother, Phil. But now that I think about it I guess he'd be, what, thirty-six, thirty-seven by now."

Phil was having a hard time staying on the road: the parked cars on the side coming out toward him; the light of the streetlamps passing overhead, fuzzy; and—damnit—why isn't that guy slowing down? Headlights were coming at an intersection. Isn't he going to stop? DAMNIT—Phil slammed on the brakes but overshot the intersection, the other car passing down the road. He pulled to the side and got out slamming the door behind him and began to walk. He should have let Warren drive him home, he thought, as he wavered down the Laurelhurst sidewalk. He shouldn't have started drinking any of the bourbon after all of the beer. But then he thought again of the federal prison and the military review board and the judge, the fucking judge, and, fuck, fuck 'em, just FUCK 'EM; he wasn't going to go fight in no fucking jungle war.

22

The waitress came up with a plate of steaming pancakes and set them on the table in front of Mitch. "No movie, Steve?" she asked the blue-denim man.

"Nah, they don't start until after four. So that takes care of that."

"I'll go get you more coffee," the pleasant-looking waitress said to Mitch, and she left again for the back.

"So, did you go to Roosevelt?" Mitch asked the denim man.

"Yeah; yeah. The Roughriders. —Hey, did you know Feldman at all?"

"Which one? I think there were a few, weren't there?"

"Scott," said the sandy-haired man.

"Scott? No; but I knew his cousin, Doug."

"Doug, yeah, hmmm, shit. Yeah, you know, I lived in Seattle my whole life, and, shit, man, that place is a bitch. But, shit, it's my home: all my family lives there, all my friends live there; I was a photographer there so all my business contacts are there…but, fuck, man, Seattle?…no thanks."

Mitch spread butter on his pancakes and then poured thick, dark syrup from the glass dispenser. Outside it began to lightly rain again as the clouds came in lower up the valley.

"Did you go to Hale?" the boyish-looking man asked Mitch.

"Yeah. Graduated in '70. How about you?"

"'71. I had a lot of friends who went to Hale, though."

Mitch stopped eating and looked up at Steve. "Did you know Kincaid?"

"No," said Steve, looking at Mitch. "But I heard what happened…"

Kincaid saw the light in the window and came up to the door of the south Seattle house and knew that this time they would have the hash. No more of this tomorrow bullshit. He knocked and the young Hispanic looking man opened the door and told him to come in. They went into the kitchen and the other man, Frank, or George, or whatever his name was, was sitting at the table tuning a small, cheap radio.

"You got the stuff?" Kincaid asked coming up.

"It's right here." The man unwadded a newspaper and slid the pound over to Kincaid and opened a drawer in a cabinet and took out a small balance scale. Kincaid put the brick on the scale and slid the weights across the arm until the plate slowly rose into the air and stopped.

"Okay—close enough," Kincaid said, and he reached into his pocket. *"Here. Two-thousand."*

The man at the table took the wad of money without counting it and then reached under the table and brought out a small handgun that he pointed at Kincaid and, grabbing the pound of hash off the scale, yelled at Kincaid to get out.

"Fuck you, man," Kincaid said very slowly, and then louder: *"What is this shit?"*

"Get back; GET THE FUCK OUT!" screamed the man with the gun. But Kincaid suddenly came at him and the man fired and then Kincaid went crazy; and it scared the man and he fired again and Kincaid went down and didn't move.

"More coffee?"

"Sure, thanks." Mitch slid his empty cup to the side of the table where the waitress stood. A couple came through the large front door and stood for a moment under the antique toboggan hanging up high on the wall above the door.

"Yeah, I went to Eckstein, and Roosevelt," the blue-denim man, Steve, said at the table, crossing his legs at his thigh and tucking a hand in between. "Sixty-fifth was the dividing line, so I had to go to Roosevelt and everybody north of sixty-fifth went to Hale. So, yeah, I knew a lot of people at Hale, too."

"I used to know a lot of those people who went to Eckstein and then Hale," said Mitch. "So I ended up meeting a lot of people from Roosevelt."

"Roosevelt was a bitch," Steve said. "Everyone I knew wanted out of there bad. So they did everything they could to get into Hale. Man, Roosevelt was like a prison; you had to work your ass off just to keep from flunking out."

"Hmmm…nah, it wasn't so bad at Hale," Mitch said. "I don't ever remember doing anything there like studying or anything. You just sort of did your time until you graduated."

"High school…" Steve shook his head.

25

The two young men sat in the old car at the back of the parking lot and smoked the joint and drank the beers and kept an eye on the entrance for the cops that came down at night to bust the teenagers who hung out in the park. Beyond the entrance the large lawns stretched down to the lake, and, except for where the tall oaks and willows and the brick bathhouse blocked their view, they could see out across the wide, choppy water to the distant shore and the glimmering lights of the houses that speckled the low hills rising up across the lake.

"Hey, keep the window down so we don't stink up the car too bad. My mother's going to be using it in the morning."

"Okay. How many beers are you going to drink?"

"I think four. But you can have one of mine if you want."

"No, I've got to get another pack of cigarettes."

"Are you almost out?"

"No, I've still got half a pack."

The young man in the passenger seat finished the joint and took out a cigarette and lit it and glanced again at the entrance. "Think if they pick my number first tomorrow."

"No!" The young man in the driver's seat gave a startled burst. "No—you don't want to think about that."

The passenger took another drink of beer. "But think if they did. Or even in the first fifty. No; you're right, I can't even think about it."

"Hey, I heard that Skale knows about some doctor who can get you four-F," said the driver. "The guy's supposed to be real cool. I guess he's already done it for a few people. But it's supposed to be real secret so Skale doesn't even know his name."

"Man, there's no way I'd ever go in even if they did pick my number," said the passenger. "No, I can't even think about it. I mean, there's just no way I could even imagine something like that. The Army. Jesus. Could you just see me or Dugan or Kincaid—Christ—Kincaid! Can you imagine some drill sergeant getting Kincaid on the first day with his hair down his back and lids stuffed all over him? Kincaid—shit! Can't you just see him trying to light up a joint in the drill line the first morning and not being able to figure out why everyone else wasn't lighting one up, too? And fuck; pushups!—'did that guy say pushups?' Jesus, Kincaid, he'd be standin' there: 'where's the music? Where's the beer?' Christ. He'd just try to walk away."

"Yeah, it'd be pretty weird all right." The driver glanced at his watch and looked again toward the dark entrance.

"Hey, let's get going. My parents have been watching me with the car a lot lately. I gotta get it back."

Outside the old lodge the rain had stopped and the clouds were now higher up the mountainsides. When the loud music playing on the stereo ended, the roar of the river near the road could be heard in the distance.

"So you going to keep working up here for a while then?" Mitch asked Steve.

"Yeah, I'm not going back to Seattle just yet, anyway. I like it here. Man, this place is beautiful."

"Yeah, it definitely is." Mitch glanced again out the tall windows. "Well, hey, I'm going to start heading back." He pushed his plate aside and picked up the check and stood up from the table. "Here, you can have the paper if you want."

"Thanks, all right. ...Hey, you didn't know Warren Kline by any chance?"

"Hmmm. No, I don't remember any Klines."

"Yeah, I guess he would have been a few years older than you."

Mitch shook his head. "Well, good luck. And nice talking to you."

"Yeah. Okay. Take it easy."

Walking out the door into the cool mountain air, Mitch saw the snow-streaked tips of the mountain peaks rising above the clouds on the far side of the valley. The roar of the river was louder, and the green of the forest beside the river and going up the steep mountainsides brighter in the mid-morning light. He got into his car and put the key into the ignition and thought of the clerical job at the downtown office where he would have to go in the morning to work, and then he thought of Kincaid losing control in the south Seattle house and being shot and dying twelve years before. Pulling out of the dirt parking lot, he started slowly down the highway as, overhead, the rain clouds again began moving in low up the valley.

If the rain holds out maybe I should stop someplace beside the river and read for a while, he thought. I could probably come close to finishing the book if I try for a while. There's sure no hurry to get back, anyway. Besides, why would anyone be in a hurry to get back to that place.

CAMPING TRIP

I

The morning air was cool in the old canvas tent when Mitchell Gray opened his eyes. Lying comfortably in his cotton sleeping bag, he listened to the distant roar of the ocean surf and watched the shadows of the forest branches move across the tent's sunlit-walls. Beside him, wrapped tightly in their bags on the large floor, Steve and Paul continued to sleep, as the flickering shadows grew slowly brighter with the rising sun.

Moving quietly, Mitch climbed out of his bag and pulled on his clothes and, unzipping the tent fly, went out into the bright forest morning. From the grassy clearing of the camp, he walked over to the edge of the high bluff and looked out at the expanse of ocean and the flat gray sand that stretched below from the tall piles of driftwood lining the base of the bluff to the distant foaming surf. Except for a light fog bank on the horizon where the ocean met the sky, there were no other clouds in the

August light, as the sun rose above the tall damp forest behind the camp.

Mitch walked back in the camp to where they had built the fire when they had arrived in darkness the night before and squatted down and stirred the still-hot ashes and laid down wadded paper and small kindling and struck a match. When the kindling caught fire he placed dry larger pieces on and felt the warmth of the flames as the thin column of smoke rose rapidly into the morning air. Walking over to the shoulder of the road to where they had left the car, he opened the trunk and took out the box of pots and pans and silverware and plates, and the food box, and carried them over to the fire where the large Coleman cooler already sat. He placed the charred metal grill over the fire and then began taking utensils and food out of the boxes and cooler to prepare breakfast.

From within the tent came the sounds of someone stirring and it shook briefly and out the door came Steve, buttoning his flannel shirt as he squinted toward Mitch in the morning light.

"Morning," said Steve in a low voice. He was not very awake.

"Hey, Steve," said Mitch, squatting by the fire with a small grin on his face. "Are you alive?"

"Heeeeey, *yeah*," Steve said in a higher voice, stretching. "I didn't sleep too bad." Finishing the buttons on his shirt, he walked over to the edge of the bluff and looked out at the ocean. "Whoa! Look at this—hey, see you in a while." And in the bright morning sun he headed down the steep bluff trail for the beach.

At the campfire, Mitch laid strips of bacon in the large black griddle and then placed it on the grill over the flames. In the far distance came the faint sound of a logging truck on the highway that ran just beyond the trees behind the camp. It was an isolated part of the coast which was the way they had wanted it, and Mitch listened beside the fire as the sound of the truck grew steadily louder until it roared past and then grew faint again and was replaced by the popping of the bacon in the griddle and the roar of the surf coming up from the beach below the bluff.

"So when do you want to hike down to the rocks?" Paul was standing beside the smoldering fire, drying the last of the plates and silverware and placing them back in the box. He had been the last to come out of the tent and seemingly the most rested. When Steve had come back from the beach, the campfire breakfast of eggs and bacon and toast was ready, and together they had sat on logs around the fire and eaten. Mitch had not minded preparing the meal; cooking food over a campfire was something he enjoyed.

"Soon. Real soon," Steve said, sounding serious as he sat by the tent in the mid-morning sun. "I can't wait to go back down there." He had been very excited since returning from the beach. "Hey, anyone know if the tide's started coming in yet?"

"Yeah, I think it has," said Mitch. He was sitting near the edge of the bluff beneath a small fir tree whose branches were badly twisted and bent toward the forest, gazing far down the beach to where a large rock point stuck out into the ocean. From time to time the white spray of heavy surf crashing into the rocks could be vaguely seen lifting into the air above the end of the point. "Well, I'm ready anytime," Mitch said as he continued to study the point. "You know, actually, we should go now, before the tide comes in too far."

"High tide's the best time to be there," said Paul. "That's when the waves are coming the farthest up the rocks. But, yeah, let's go now so we can still see some tidal pools."

"Hey, you guys ever been to the cave that's there?" Mitch asked from the edge of the bluff.

"Not me," said Steve.

"Man, you wouldn't believe this cave," Mitch went on. "But you can only see it at low tide. I remember seeing it once with my family when I was a kid. It's actually more like a tunnel, though, really. You go into it from the beach side and then come out the other end and you're right above where the surfs hitting the rocks. And then when the tide comes in the waves start coming right through the tunnel."

"Really?" said Steve, and he stood up from the ground and brushed off his pants. "Sounds cool. So why don't we get going then before the tide comes in much more?"

"Yeah, let's head out," said Paul, stirring up the ashes of the fire. "And we can definitely look for some tidal pools."

Steve and Mitch put the boxes beside the cooler and Paul zipped up the tent and one at a time they scrambled down the steep bluff trail to the beach.

Mitch was running on the dark sand now, several miles down the beach, coming up to the rocky point that protruded into the ocean like the tail of a huge dragon, the scaly but climbable wall-like edge rising up suddenly out of the flat sand. The point rose higher as it extended into the ocean, almost becoming an island at high tide, and then dropped off steeply into the water where the waves battered the end like slow moving rams, sending thick walls of spray high into the air. Back at the base of the bluff were huge piles of sun-bleached logs—their long journeys from the banks of distant river valleys temporarily stalled—which deepened greatly where the rock point left the bluff. Following the point's steep sides, the incoming waves flowed smoothly along the rock face, breaking only where an uneven section protruded. From behind him in the distance down the gray-sand beach, the two figures of Paul and Steve approached rapidly through the occasional mist drifting in off the ocean. Encompassing all was the constant roar of surf.

"I don't see it anywhere!" Mitch yelled when they were almost upon him. He followed the rock wall toward the water until he found some handholds and then climbed quickly onto a low ledge just as a thin tongue of surf came swiftly in, sweeping over his footprints in the sand. From the ledge he looked out to the outcropping of rocks which now blocked his view of the heaviest outer surf, and, climbing higher, made his way up to the crest. From there he could see the sand beach continuing on to another rock point and beyond it another, and the rocky coastline curving far into the distance, and, rising out of the water just beyond the next point, like the gnarled fingers of an old man's hand, a great field of wave-battered seastacks, extending up the coastline for as far as he could see. And everywhere was the glistening green of wet seaweed and hundreds of small water-filled tidal pools carpeted thickly with barnacles and tiny crabs, and, farther out, bright orange and purple starfish on the sides of the deeper pools and covering the bottoms, spiny, donut-shaped sea anemones, all in the clear salty water of the pools.

"Hey, Mitch!" the call came from below, piercing the damp air over the roar of the surf.

"Up here!" He could see them now scrambling up the rocks toward him. They made it up to the crest and stood beside him looking up the coastline and the endless series of protruding points and the fields of seatacks rising out of the water.

"Jesus shit! This is *unreal!*" Steve shouted over the roar of the surf. He was standing in the damp breeze, grinning; he looked happy. Over a ways, Paul squatted before an anemone-filled pool.

"Whoa," said Paul in a serious tone, looking deep into the clear water, "look at the size of some of these."

Mitch and Steve leaped over to Paul and looked down at the bright orange and green sea anemones lining the bottom. There was a silent calm in the pool, unlike the immediate area where the ocean met the land and was anything but quiet and calm.

"I still don't see the cave," said Mitch, looking out the point. "I'm not even sure if it's still there." He leaped to another slab of rock and continued toward the tall island-like mound, following a ledge that angled down to a sandy spot near the water on the other side of the crest. There a ring of large rocks just off shore protected the water from the waves and he continued on the sand until it ended at a deep pool and he had to climb back onto the rocks in order to keep going. Leaping and bounding along a few yards behind, Steve and Paul followed Mitch's route out the dark point.

Rounding a narrow ledge just above the waterline, Mitch stopped and looked down at a wide sandbar at the base of the island-end. "Son-of-a-bitch!" he yelled out. "There it is!...I think... Yeah! Right down there!" He was pointing toward a dark spot where the sandbar disappeared into the rock face. He made his way to above the sandbar and leaped down and walked in the soft sand to where the cut in the rocks began and, crouching down to clear the low opening, disappeared into the rocks.

It was light inside the cave which passed completely through the point's tall end and opened onto the other side, and quiet, as the roar of the ocean was now only a faint noise in the distance. A pool of water filled the bottom and only by following a ring of protruding rocks could he make his way further into the dome-shaped tunnel and toward the sunlight coming through the far opening. Crouched over from the curving wall above his head, Mitch stopped for a moment on a rock and listened to the roar of individual waves hitting the point from out the tunnel's seaward end. Just below the waterline—as though from eternity—starfish, with their bloated orange points, clung to the dark walls and beside the starfish thick clusters of dark-blue muscle shells and everywhere huge white barnacles; and it was quiet and peaceful now but he knew it wouldn't be later when the waves began coming in and the tunnel filled with the cold water of the ocean. Making his way deeper into the chasm, the sound of the waves hitting out the seaward side grew steadily louder until he reached the opening and climbed out onto a ledge and back into the sunlight; and everywhere now the waves roared loudly into the steep point-walls and then it was suddenly quiet until the sheets of spray floating in the air showered down heavily onto the rocks around him. He was standing in a kind of channel that came far into the point toward the tunnel, with tall, sunlit-walls to one side and behind, and a flat lower ledge of rocks before him leading out into the sea. After a wave came crashing in and the spray had fallen, there followed the long sound of draining water from high off the channels rocks and ledges as the sea lowered until the next wave came and filled the channel again. Mitch walked farther out the ledge, almost to the end where it dropped off into the sea; and he was surrounded by water on three sides: the channel was on one side and on the other the con-

tinuing coastline of protruding points and seastacks and before him the open ocean, and he sat down on the ledge. Now he was surrounded everywhere by the heavy roar of surf onto rocks and the showering of spray and he could see how the waves came in and over the rocks and which rocks were safe and others close by that were not safe now and never would be again for land-based creatures; and a large wave came into the ledge and sent spray high into the air and onto Mitch. But he could see that the ledge was safe for now, that it was dry—except for what had just happened with that last wave— and then he saw an even better rock that was closer still to the rising and low-ering ocean and he knew that it would be an even better view of the tall point and the rocks and the sunlit coast and the very high vertical lifting of water. But he also knew that it would not be a very good place to stay for very long and that maybe he should watch it for a while to better see exactly what was going on with its unusually wet surface and the cold sea around it. But suddenly the water drained unpredictably low around the nearest part and he quickly jumped up and leaped out onto the rock and scrambled hurriedly up to the highest point. Now he was in the ocean but on the rock but feeling as much of the heavy surf as he could without being in it; and it surrounded him completely and he had to keep close track of all the heavily moving water that was everywhere and he did keep track of it—or it of him. But now suddenly he felt very guilty about the unpredictably large wave that was rapidly approaching for having such an unserious attitude about harm and the great disappointment he would now cause his family for having done another bad thing: gone away for good without letting them know where he was or when he'd be home. And he knew he'd probably be hurting them the most ever this time, and that he would probably be badly punished—restricted or something—and he crouched far over and tucked his head down and held onto the wet surface as best he could as the wave hit and came unpredictably high onto the rock. And a huge wall of spray drove down hard and onto Mitch and he grinned widely in deep guilt when he knew that the wave had not been too unpredictable. And, soaked to the bone, he spun quickly and scrambled back down and leaped with all his strength back to the cave-ledge; and now he felt nothing but very deep, unpredictable guilt.

"Yeah! Mitch!—HEY!" the sharp cries of Steve's voice pierced the air as Steve and Paul climbed out of the tunnel and onto the ledge. "Whoa—shit! This is outrageous!" Steve yelled over the roar of the waves as he and Paul made their way toward Mitch who was squatted down at the end of the ledge. More loudly than ever was the heavy rising and lowering of water onto rocks; and a wall of spray showered down hard onto the ledge between Steve and Paul and onto Paul. Now moving quickly out the ledge, Steve leaped toward Mitch and then stopped. "Jesus Christ! Did you fall in?"

Mitch smiled weakly and looked at the rock where he had just been. "No. A wave got me." The rock was taking water heavily now and then suddenly the water drained completely off and it sat silently in the sunlight surrounded by the dark sea. Making his way out the ledge, Paul came excitedly up to Steve and Mitch. "Damn! I'm wet. Hey," he looked at Mitch still squatting on the rock, "man, you're soaked!"

"Yeah, I went way out there." Mitch's clothes were very wet and his hair and face wet and he took off his glasses and tried to dry them but everything was wet.

"*Whoa!*" Steve suddenly yelled, and they all three saw the large wave at the same time that was rapidly approaching the point and Mitch jumped up first and they all moved quickly back to the middle of the ledge and then turned to watch the force of the wave hit the point and wash over the end of the ledge and fill the channel deeper than any wave they had seen before; and the spray showered down long and hard and together they heard the first short draining into the tunnel of the incoming tide.

38

II

"Hey, when do you want to take these?" Paul stood at the door of the tent with the three capsules of mescaline in his hand.

Mitch looked up from beside the coals of the fire where he finished drying the last plate from the steak dinner that he, Paul and Steve had just finished eating. "Huh... you brought some caps...from Breener?"

Paul and Steve knew Bret and Bret knew Breener and Breener always had the best of that sort of thing and people were always glad about the things that Breener could get them and Breener was glad they were glad and everyone was glad.

"Yep," said Paul, now examining closely the small blue capsules in his hand. "At least I'm pretty sure."

"Huh, well, maybe I'll take a half," said Mitch. "How long do they last?"

"I don't know," said Paul. "I actually haven't had any of these, but Steve thought they were just like what Bret had in June. And those you started getting off in about half an hour and then peaked for about three hours and then you just stayed high for, I don't know, about six or eight."

"Huh...well...yeah. I guess so," Mitch said. "You can split 'em, can't you? Yeah, I just want a half."

A noise came from back in the woods and out of the trees came Steve with a large armful of wood that he threw onto the pile by the almost-out-fire. "There."

"Hey, Steve, when do you want to take these?" Paul asked, stepping out of the tent and holding out his hand to show Steve what he had.

"Hey—all right—yeah. Let's go—I'm ready! You guys ready? Mitch?"

"Yeah, well, I just want a half."

"A half," said Steve. "Yeah, well, that'll still get you off. It's supposed to be pretty clean. From Breener."

"Yeah, actually, Steve, I don't think I want a whole, either," said Paul.

"Yeah, well, all right. I think Bret just took a half once and got off pretty good. How about if we split two of them up three ways and then there won't be any left over and I won't be the only one taking a whole?"

"Sounds good to me," said Paul, taking out his pocketknife and walking over to the box with the plates beside the cooler.

"Yeah, okay," said Mitch, and he got up and walked over to the bluff. Draped over a tree branch were his still damp clothes catching the last rays of the sun sinking now toward the ocean which spread out immensely below the bluff. The sky was clear and the air warm and Mitch looked out at the early evening view. In the distance he saw the rock point, illuminated by the setting sun, but only vaguely could he make out the crashing waves. And in the other direction, even further down the beach, in front of the Forest Service Campground, he could see the tiny figures of people walking on the wide sand which spread out greatly now with the low tide.

"Hey, Mitch!" Paul yelled from back in the camp. "—Okay."

The figures down the beach were larger now as Mitch, Steve, and Paul moved across the wide sand toward the Forest Service Campground. The sun was sinking rapidly toward the water and the darkening sky remained clear and calm. In front of them, the coastline extended immensely, as well as behind, with the rolling ocean on one side and the flat sand on the other leading up to the driftwood and bluff and the tall forest and beyond the forest the foothills rising into the mountains.

They walked side by side, close to the thin tongues of surf that came rolling far up the sand, toward the figures down the beach who seemed to be gathering at a single spot near the edge of the driftwood. Now they saw the thin column of smoke rising rapidly into the air and the ring of logs and the people gathering at the ring, and they began to angle slowly away from the water and toward the fire.

They slowed their pace across the sand as they approached the people who were all moving about. Mitch noticed that they moved differently from the way the sand and the ocean and the forest moved. They were all moving, but in a different way. He knew that people moved, like from walking or moving their arms, or even from moving their mouths when talking, and he knew that the water and the sand and the trees moved when the wind blew, but he didn't know that they also moved when there was no wind; and he watched them move everywhere in the very still air.

I didn't know that.

The air moved, too, though; a vague swirl of color. It was also the largest part of all the things around him: larger even than the sea or sand or the forest, or the people up ahead who were all moving a lot, but differently, and now talking; but the air, the largest part, moved the most.

I didn't know that.

"Steve!" Mitch called out to Steve who was stopped a ways in front of him, studying the people at the fire. Now Mitch grinned. He hadn't expected the 'Steve' he heard that had come out of his mouth. *"Hay, Stave,"* he called again, grinning. *"How do you like the sky?"*

"Whot?"

Mitch also hadn't expected the 'what' he heard come out of Steve's mouth, either. It was not a 'what' he had expected. He had expected a higher 'what' and not a low 'what'—like a record spinning too slowly—that Steve had given him. *That was not a 'what' I had expected, he thought. Or 'whot'. Shit: 'whot!' 'Whot, whot, whot'. But I hadn't expected the people to be moving so differently from the way the sand and the air moved, either. That's something else I didn't know.*

Whot?

"Match!" Paul was calling out from behind Mitch where he had drifted the furthest back. Now he was talking funny; and Mitch turned and grinned at him as Paul came up close, also grinning.

This grinning's killing me, Mitch thought, and he burst out laughing.

Paul was now up very close to Mitch, grinning widely, and Mitch noticed that Paul's face looked different, especially the skin.

I didn't know that.

It seemed kind of paler, and more textured, but not really but kind of but not really.

Whot?

It was more textured, though, and—*whaaahhhht?* it was moving.

Mitch stopped laughing, but kept grinning at Paul, who was also grinning, very widely, as widely as Mitch had ever seen anyone grin before, to where he thought that Paul's grin was stretching out wider than his face, especially the corners of his mouth and teeth, but not really, but yes kind of, but yes really; and moving.

"Mitch, can you believe the sky?" Paul said, grinning.

Mitch turned and saw the sun, red and large, sinking through a narrow line of clouds into the ocean.

Going, going, going.

It was still only a third down.

Going, going.

There was a lot of unusual movement everywhere, except for the sun, which was moving as it always did.

Going.

The sky moved immensely, like a great flowing pattern; the water moved strangely, rapidly off to the sides; the sand swirled briskly about; but the sun moved normally: down. Slowly. Sinking.

Gone.

Now the sky turned red and the Earth's shadow moved up the forest covered hills toward the mountains which could not be seen behind the hills, and Mitch, grinning only slightly, and then not at all, turned away from the water and looked again at Paul's textured, moving face. "So, Paul, how are you getting off? Pretty good?" Mitch asked.

"Gyeah," said Paul up close. "Gyeah, I'd have to say so." And he grinned again, an enormous moving grin. "Hey…hey come on. Let's see what's up here." And with a great movement of his arm he gestured toward the people up the beach.

"Yeah. Okay."

They walked up the sand toward Steve who was waiting for them, grinning, near the edge of the driftwood, just before the crowd of people gathered at the ring of logs around the fire. There were maybe twenty people sitting and standing around the large campfire, all of them either older adults or parents with young children. They were also moving.

A lot.

"What the hell?" said Paul.

"Huh…" Steve said.

"What do think it is?" said Mitch.

"Man, I'm not sure," Paul said.

"Huh…beats me," Steve said. "Maybe a party."

Whot?

"Yeah!" said Paul, grinning widely again.

"Hey—look," said Steve. "A Ranger."

Now they saw a man in a Forest Service uniform moving about the fire, placing on large logs, building it up higher and higher, until the wood crackled and sparked loudly with flames as the column of smoke rose rapidly into the darkening sky.

"Gyeah. Come on," said Steve.

Walking quickly up the heavily moving sand from where they stood a short ways away, they came to the moving ring of logs and sat on one that was still and tried not to draw any attention to themselves and avoided looking at anyone's eyes; but Mitch couldn't help looking. He tried not to, though, but he couldn't help looking at all the heavily textured faces; especially the children's. He tried, though; but, well, there are unusual faces, and heavily textured ones, and faces that are difficult to look at on vast ocean beaches in the early evening, but the faces of the small children playing in the sand around the fire were the worst.

Didn't know that.

And ugly.

Whot?

And they were not caring what anyone thought of them and their extremely undeveloped faces. They were sort of not human—at least in the way they acted and drew so much attention. But they looked human, except for their somewhat pinkish, no red, no white faces, and their unusual shapes which seemed more beast-like than human; and Mitch tried to look away. But they drew so much attention that he had to look again, and he did, grinless, as he sat on the log beside Paul and Steve trying not to draw any attention.

This is the strangest party.

But the children were the most strange, drawing tremendous amounts of attention—especially from the parents—and not caring about how they looked: human or beast. A little boy beast played with a stick in the sand near Mitch, and, just beyond, a little girl beast held on to the moving, trousered legs of her mother; and the little girl looked strangely at Mitch and Mitch looked quickly up at the tremendously moving sky. She moved an awful lot, too, though, and strangely, and was not very attractive, and the boy-beast, her brother, making the most unusual sounds, plowed sand all about and got it everywhere. He was getting it on himself and on his sister and some flew onto Mitch; and the boy suddenly stopped and looked at Mitch, and Mitch looked at the fire.

What?

The people were talking strangely, too; mostly the parents to the furry beasts, trying to keep them under control. The children definitely seemed to want to move around a lot, and act out in unusual ways, not caring about drawing attention.

No; definitely didn't know that.

Sitting very still on the log amongst the ring of people, the three of them said nothing as the ranger stood up from placing wood onto the now roaring fire. They did not want to speak to anyone to find out what was going on because they did not want to bring any attention to themselves; but it sure seemed they stood out. It seemed they stood out immensely, like large hairy beasts, or at least like the brilliantly moving sky, and they tried not to grin. The children stood out the most, though. They were definitely unusual little creatures.

The fire blazed brightly and the sky darkened and the ranger stepped back and said that it was now time to begin, and, in a soft, deep voice, very slowly began to sing a song. And the closely huddled ring of greatly textured people, their moving faces glowing heavily in the raging light of the fire, began in loud, near-perfect unison to sing along. And Mitch, Steve, and Paul got quickly up and without looking back moved briskly across the dark sand in the direction from which they had come.

III

"Jee-sus Kir-IST!" Steve was laughing loudly in front of the fire at the camp. "It was too much. Just—too—*much!*"

"Insane," said Paul excitedly. "Totally, unbelievably, insane."

It was all they had talked about in the hour it had taken to walk back in the darkness to the camp and rebuild the fire: the people, the ranger, the singing.

"Yeah. Wow. Hey, is anybody still getting off?" Steve asked, quieter, now only grinning.

"A little," said Paul, also quieter.

"Yeah, you know it's not bad stuff," said Steve, "but now I think I'm almost completely down." He looked at Paul, grinning wider, and began laughing again: "God! Just too much." He got up from the ground, laughing, and walked over to the edge of the bluff and stared out into the darkness and became quiet. The sky was black, but for an occasional star and a sliver of moon, which lit vaguely the wide surface of the shimmering sea. Up from the beach came the roar of surf, filling the cool night air.

"Man, that was just incredible," said Paul, back at the fire. "—I still can't believe it."

"Yeah, I know," said Mitch.

"God, those people!" said Paul.

"Those kids," said Mitch.

"Insane."

"Yeah—man, I was really getting off."

"God, I was hallucinating insanely," said Paul. "…Just insanely."

They were only hallucinating a little now, though. Actually almost not at all because now they were only getting off a little. Hallucinating is what they did a lot, though, when they were getting off a lot. Hallucinate; hallucinate; hallucinate. Insanely. Everything; everywhere; all over the place. Back and forth; to the sides; in and out. But then gradually everything came back to normal and they only hallucinated a little and then not at all.

"Hey, are you still getting off?" Mitch asked. He was wondering if Paul was still seeing unusual things.

Paul studied the fire for a moment and then the glow on the tree trunks surrounding the camp and the shadows going back into the forest. "...Just a little. Actually, I don't know. Hardly at all. Are you?"

Mitch looked around briefly. Then he held his hand out at arms length and swung it across his face. "...No, not really. Well, maybe some. I guess." Now he looked far into the glowing coals and thought about the children and the voices of the parents and how strange they had all seemed. Then a breeze moved across the tops of the trees and he reached over and pushed a log further into the fire and watched the sparks shoot rapidly into the dark air.

"Man, too bad it wasn't a party," said Paul in the glow of the fire, leaning back on his elbows on the ground. "I was really hoping we'd find something going on."

"Yeah," said Mitch. "...I don't know, usually you can find people getting off at the ocean, somewhere. I don't know...it's just better."

"Yeah. Really. A lot better," said Paul. "Everything. It all just makes more sense."

"Yeah. It's not so paranoid. You can just get off. But, shit, too bad we didn't run into something."

"Yeah. A little wine," said Paul.

"Some grass."

"Yeah."

Mitch looked up from the fire. "Hey, I have a little chunk of hash."

"No kidding? Really? What kind?"

"Looks like black to me," said Mitch, and he got up from the ground and went over to the tent. Paul remained beside the fire, looking at the flames that flickered into the air from the burning logs.

From the edge of the bluff, Steve called back to the camp, "Hey, did I hear somebody say hash?"

"Yeah, Mitch said he's got some."

"*—In here,*" Mitch yelled from the tent, and Steve, re-appearing from the bluff, and Paul, getting up from the ground, went into the tent and dropped down on their bags beside Mitch who was poking at the bowl of a small metal pipe with a pin as he drew on the stem to check the air flow.

It was dark inside the tent, but for the flashlight which lay turned on in a corner on the floor, and the flickering light of the campfire a few feet away coming through the open flap. Beside Mitch on the canvas floor lay a small open wad of tinfoil with two finger-thick chunks of a dark, soft-looking substance. A box of stick matches lay beside the foil.

"Hey—it's black," said Steve, carefully picking up the foil.

"Yeah, I'm pretty sure," said Mitch, still working on the pipe, "It's from Lyle." Now he took one of the chunks from the foil and placed it in the bowl and handed the pipe to Paul and picked up the box of matches and took one out. He struck the match against the side of the box and it burst into flame, releasing a small cloud of sulfur, and held the flame to Paul who drew deeply on the narrow stem. As the flame drew over the dark chunk, it began to turn red around the edges and then released a thin column of smoke into the air when Paul, his face contorted from the depth of his breath, removed the stem from his lips. Now Steve took the pipe as Mitch held the still burning match up to the bowl. Steve blew as much air from his lungs as he could, then inhaling very slowly and deeply, began to draw on the pipe. Leaning back on his arms on the tent floor as he struggled to keep the burning smoke in his lungs, Paul tilted his head toward the ceiling and began to choke sharply as he let out a thick, seemingly-endless column of smoke, followed by a loud violent cough. Now Mitch drew deeply on the still burning chunk until his face turned red and shook; and he handed the pipe back to Paul who drew in the remaining small amount of smoke as the chunk turned completely red and then went out. Now Mitch and Steve, also bursting from the intensely expanding heat in their lungs, blew out the hot smoke in long gasping chokes.

"Man…" said Steve, very softly, his eyes red and moist.

"Yeah," said Paul, quietly, struggling to sit up.

Things were beginning to change.

"…Hmmm…well…" Steve now said, slightly louder, looking at the remaining chunk in the foil.

"Yeah…" said Paul.

"Whoa…" said Mitch, somewhat hoarsely, not looking at anyone.

Still staring at the foil, Steve took the last chunk and with a slight tremble set it in the pipe; and Paul struck another match and held it up to the bowl as Steve began to draw again from the stem. Now he began to choke almost immediately; and in the dim light he let out another thick cloud of billowing smoke and then began to cough violently again as his eyes watered more. "Go, Mitch," Paul said, still holding the burning match in his also trembling hand.

First emptying his lungs with all his strength, Mitch took the heavily smoking pipe and—*Jessus*—began to draw slowly and—*Jee-zus*—deeply on the stem as—*whoa*—the small chunk glowed bright—*hmmmm*—very bright, almost differently...*I didn't know that.*

Now, now, now...oh, shit... Well... Whot?...

As Mitch blew the smoke from his lungs, the changes began to occur rapidly and a lot, an awful lot; not like the city: recent and small; but like the ocean and the sky: old and big; and the mountains just inland that could only be seen at times through the deep cuts of the river valleys: soaring upward. Mostly it was the stretching. The stretching of the faces. The stretching of Paul's face, first, from across the tent where he sat quietly in the dim light, to over near Mitch: a long pointing stretch of the face clear across the tent. And then Steve's: first out a few feet, and then back in almost all the way, and then slowly out again, long and pointed, more pointed than the jagged tips of the nearby peaks, clear across the tent; and Mitch held on to his sleeping bag and tried to think about the crashing waves and the spray on the rocks. But the harder he tried, the more things changed; and then the texture and color of the stretching faces of his two good friends became like chowder, and he grasped the cloth of the bag with a fury and held on for his dear, dear life.

51

He awoke lying through the door of the tent in the early morning light, his upper half on the ground outside and the rest of him inside the tent on the sleeping bag. The sun was rising behind the trees in the cool morning air, and the shadows of the branches and leaves flickered about the ground around him. Coming from the beach in the distance below the bluff was the roar of the surf filling the salty air. Still in his clothes from the night before, Mitch pulled himself out the tent door and stood in the clearing of the camp. Now he looked through the dark trunks of the trees to the car, caked with dirt and still sitting on the side of the road where they had left it the night they had arrived; and he walked over and stood beside the dead ashes and charred wood of the fire. From inside the tent came a soft stirring and emerging slowly out the door was Steve, buttoning his flannel shirt and squinting into the morning light. "Whew…shit," he said softly, his voice cracking.

"…Shit," said Mitch quietly, glancing toward Steve.

"…How's it going, Mitch?" Steve asked, moving slowly toward the charred pit.

"I don't know. Okay…I guess."

"Man, I thought you were gone."

Mitch didn't say anything.

"It took a little longer to hit us…but…shit…" And Steve turned toward the bluff and looked out at the sea.

"Yeah…I don't know…" Mitch said in a kind of muffled voice that Steve really didn't hear. *I don't know a thing, a thang, a fucking thang,* he thought, standing in the filtering light of the forest. *Except that I've got to get the car back by tonight and find Lyle and talk to Jeff about the dishwashing job, and...well...I don't know...* "Hey, what do you say we get going before long?" he called to Steve. "It's a three hour drive. I don't want to get back real late."

Steve looked up from the bluff. "Yeah. Fine with me. I wouldn't mind trying to get a few things done at home tonight... Well, unless you want to try and go up the Quinault. Nah, on second thought let's get going."

"Yeah. We can do the Quinault another time," said Mitch. "So why don't you go wake up Paul and let's go." And Steve headed to the tent and Mitch picked up one of the boxes and began to carry it through the trees to the car.

FIORINI SKI SCHOOL

"Look, Mommy, Daddy's staring at an old truck again. He always does that."

"I know, sweetheart, Daddy's being funny again. He likes the smell. He likes that yukky smoke."

It was the diesel fuel and Issac York could not help it. Like flipping a switch, the smell of the smoke delivered him back in time, back to eighth grade and the parking lot of the Snoqualmie Summit ski area in the heart of the Cascade Mountains in Washington State. It delivered him there whether he wanted to go or not, where the scores and scores of buses for Saturday ski school, including the ones from Fiorini, unloaded and picked up the hundreds and hundreds of shrieking adolescents from the Seattle area for the day's classes on the gently rising slopes.

The idling engines of all those diesel buses, jammed like sardines into the parking lot, with just enough space for the storage doors to be yanked open, the skis and poles pulled out, and the heavily-clothed, hyper-excited students to make their way to the assembly area beside the lodge. A thick cloud of diesel smoke emanating from the lot, mixed and inhaled with the cold mountain air by the screaming, puffing throng, permeating the thick layers of clothing so they still reeked in the pile on the bedroom floor in the middle of the next week.

The smell took Issac back to the empty parking lot of University Village in front of the old Fiorini store, in the foggy darkness of the early Saturday morning, where the half-dozen Fiorini buses, idling, smoking, picked up the mostly silent, still-awakening students, shuttled in from the surrounding neighborhoods in station wagons and big sedans, by an almost equally bleary-eyed procession of parents for the hour long ride to the summit.

"But why does he have to stare, Mommy? Daddy's weird!"

"Daddy is weird sometimes, sweetheart. He's just re-membering."

He remembered the buses, all right—the smoke made sure of that—and he remembered the eventually-scream-ing kids during the ride (usually at full volume by the time they got to Issaquah), but he also remembered the attractive young ski instructors, students from the Uni-versity, who were the chaperones on the buses and had to keep things under control. He remembered how they weren't quite adults, more like older brothers and sisters, but still with kid-like qualities, trying to mix the job and its responsibilities with a day of fun on the slopes.

And then he would remember Linda and Dan.

"Do you think she's a model?" Peter Burling asked Issac York in the back of the bus, where they engaged their junior high-school conversation over the loud whine of the engine and even louder chatter of the passengers.

"She's got to be, I think I've even seen her in some magazines for ski clothes, or somewhere."

Toward the front, leaning back to console a nearly-crying girl—her expression as peaceful and calming as the deep blanket of snow that covered the shoulders and forest beside the road—Linda Cambell, nineteen years old, University sophomore, silently moved her parted lips, her short, straight blond hair perfect, like her teeth and nose and eyes and hands, and how the rest of her, underneath the sweaters and parkas and pants, must, undoubtedly, be. She was like nothing Peter or Issac had ever seen before, and they silently thanked their parents for having accidentally arranged this experience.

Two seats up, a big kid hit a smaller kid.

"Franklin…don't make me come back there… Do not make me come back there." Across the aisle from Linda, where he was every week, Dan Duncan, twenty-one years old, university senior, turned quickly and glared menacingly at the bigger kid, who smiled lamely—the gap of a recently lost tooth adding to the child's already-immense troublemaking air—as Linda turned and placed a hand on Dan's arm, whom she feared would scare the boy.

Now the driver was scolding a kid near the front who had somehow rolled over the back of his seat bench and tumbled into the aisle as the bus bounced noisily up the highway. Rising quickly, Dan dragged the kid back to his seat, creating a roar from the students that drowned out the sound of the engine.

Linda got up also and made her way to the front and spoke briefly to the driver, squeezing past Dan who was talking sternly to the young acrobat. Without looking, he put his hand on Linda when she passed by. Linda was Dan's girlfriend. And they may as well have been from another planet, as their romantic asides seemed overwhelmingly unworldly, like two characters out of a movie. A Saturday afternoon movie.

"You gonna go up *Thunderbird* at lunch?" Peter asked Issac, evenly, facing the front, as they both watched Linda return to her seat.

"Yeah, think so."

When they pulled into the snow-rutted parking lot— now in a line of buses that curved back down the highway and peeled off in front at the direction of the flagger—Issac and Peter, and everyone else on board, began to pull on the mittens and scarves and goggles and hats they had carried in their laps, while trying, with mixed results, to remain seated, like Dan had loudly lectured before setting off from the Village when they had first taken their seats.

Linda looked at Dan, who had turned with dagger-eyes to observe the results of his talk. "Cindy... Greg— *GREG—GR...*" before he could say it again, everyone was out of their seats and in the aisle and reaching for their bags in the overhead racks, just as the bus rolled to a stop. Now Dan stood, too, along with Linda, and they retrieved their bags and joined the swift flow exiting the bus.

"Come on, Daddy, let's go, it's starting to rain... Mommy, it's starting to rain!"

"Issac...we're getting in the car."

"Be right there."

Issac York stood for a moment under the gray sky beside where the old truck continued to spew smoke from its exhaust. Diesel smoke, as the first drops of rain began to tap rings into a nearby puddle.

The next year Dan was gone. Linda was there in the bus again, and one of the other instructors—the school seemed even bigger: more buses; more students; more instructors—but no Dan. It was hard to notice at first, but Linda did not seem as happy, not as serene. She was as beautiful as ever—a year older, even more so—but she seemed distantly troubled, at times looking out the window on the way up, something she had seemed never to do the year before: a distant look of worry partially concealed behind the reassuring smile that was a part of her job.

By the third week we learned that over the summer Dan had been sent to Viet Nam. We all knew about Viet Nam, in the way that fourteen year olds know about the world beyond their families and homes: vaguely; fleetingly; insignificantly. The ski season was long: Firorini's lasting from early December to late April, and by the middle of January we had mostly forgotten about Dan, the bus as loud and chaotic as ever. Linda seemed to become her old self again, too, smiling more, laughing, content and happy. By February we saw her walking with one of the other male instructors. They were holding hands.

"Hey, you see Linda today? She was holding hands with Carl!" Peter blurted to Issac as they returned to the bus after the day's lessons.

"Yeah, I saw 'em after we got back last week—she got into his 'Vette. And listen to this: Karen Potts—her older sister's one of the instructors—she says Linda sent Dan this letter. It's called a *'Dear John'* letter."

"Yeah?"

"Yeah, I guess it's how girls break up with guys when they go in the Army."

"Really?"

"Yeah."

As the diesel truck pulled out, Issac York breathed the last of the fumes.

"Issac…you're getting wet…we're leaving…"

"Okay, okay, coming, coming." He stood for a moment, then with the rain falling harder, turned and walked toward his family in the car.

"What the fuck's with Danny? Is he goddamn crying? Holy fuck."

"Hey, leave him alone…he got a letter from his old lady yesterday…she cast him off."

"That one he writes to six times a week?"

"*You shoulda heard him last night...*"

"*Fuck...*"

"*All right you ugly motherfuckers: packs on, ammo out; Charlie's waitin' for us up this road, and we aint gonna disappoint.*"

THE HUSKIES

I liked those mornings when the Huskies were going to play and you didn't have to worry or anything about what to do. It was football so of course it was fall and usually kind of cloudy out, but mostly I remember it being windy from after a rain, and wet, and the trees and hills and buildings wet and everything kind of gray and the sky gray except for the quick patches of blue that might open up if it was real windy and the rain clouds were moving overhead fast.

And of course it was Saturday so I could take it easy for most of the morning because the game wouldn't be starting until one or so and Dad wouldn't be coming over until eleven or so and if I'd been out real late the night before having a good time or something, I'd have slept it off pretty much and not been rushed getting up early; but I never woke up bad or anything.

"Hey, Mitch, it's for you, your Dad."

In those days after high school I usually had a room-mate and lived in some old apartment somewhere around town and worked a little and took community college classes and tried to figure out what I was going to do for the next month and the rest of my life and all that shitty stuff you always had to think about after high school when you didn't have the damnedest idea of what you wanted to do or if the crazy old world was still even going to be around in a few years to do anything in. But on Saturdays in the fall when the Huskies were playing you didn't have to worry about any of that and that felt good.

"Yeah? Morning. Okay. Okay, all right. Okay. Good bye."

Dad usually called to make sure about when he'd be over and to say that Mom was packing sandwiches and hot chocolate and to tell me the weather report and to wear something warm because it would get cold in the upper deck, even though I knew it would get cold and he knew I knew because we'd been going to the games since I was a little kid, but he always said to anyway. I guess he'd just want to make sure.

"You got a ticket to the game?"

My roommate would usually ask, even though they usually knew that was probably why my Dad had called; but sometimes they didn't know me that well, although I had probably mentioned it sometime during the week. Back then, the Huskies were the only game, back before all the people started moving in and it got big and crowded.

"Yeah, it's Stanford, they'll probably get killed."

In those days they always lost and never went to the Rose Bowl or anything. They were just the Huskies and this was just Seattle. It wasn't California or anything. It wasn't a very famous or important place or anywhere that anyone knew anything about. It just rained here a lot. Why would anyone come here?

So usually by around eleven or so Dad would come by and pick me up and we'd make our way down to the 'U' District and over to the hospital because that's where Dad was a doctor, and he had a sticker on the car so we could park in the hospital lot which was right across the street from the stadium.

"I've got to check on a couple of patients, Mitch. Do you want to come up? We've still got plenty of time."

After we parked the car we'd usually go into the hospital through the old basement door in back and up to the eighth floor where most of Dad's patients were, and he'd usually check in on someone or give a report or something to someone.

"I won't be long."

I didn't like hospitals much but that one was different because it was Dad's and I could go places in it with him that you usually couldn't go, and I wasn't going to have anything done to me or anything because there wasn't anything wrong with me, and I could just look. Usually I'd just walk up the ward while he checked on someone.

"Good morning, Don. How are you doing today? Did Nancy get you on the treadmill okay?"

I could usually see him talking to someone he was trying to rehabilitate. That's what he did, rehabilitate. They had usually been in a car wreck or something and been injured pretty bad and he was trying to help them to move again.

"Oh, yes, good morning, Doctor, yes, we went on it, we went on it. She said I did good, that I did good."

"I'm glad to hear that. There was a message that your sister would be coming up from San Francisco next week. Did you get that?"

"Oh, no, no, I didn't hear. Okay, okay."

Actually, the ones on Dad's floor had been hurt real bad and would never be the same again. Most of them were paralyzed. Sometimes he'd just say beforehand that he was going to see someone that was paralyzed. He said some of them couldn't move their legs or their arms. He said they were quadriplegics.

It was pretty quiet up there on the eighth floor on Saturday mornings because most of the doctors and staff worked during the week except for a few nurses and orderlies, and you could just look around at all the equipment.

But usually after a while I'd walk down to the end of the hall where the window on the fire escape door was, and I could look down onto Portage Bay and the boats, and the big tour boats packed with people going to the game, and above the canal the tall, wet cement of the freeway bridge.

"Okay, Mitch, let's go."

"Is he going to be all right?"

"I don't know."

"What happened to him?"

"His spinal chord was severed in an accident at work. He's a nice man. He won't have any movement in his legs anymore. He'll probably be with us for a few more months, and then he'll go home. The way it looks is he'll regain some of the movement in his arms. ...Here, hold these."

So with all the things we were carrying to the game we'd go back down the elevator and make our way out of the building and usually see a few more people along the way that Dad knew, and he'd smile when he saw them and stop and talk to them for a minute and introduce me and then we'd get going again.

It was crowded outside by now with the time to kick-off closer and usually still windy and everyone moving on over to the stadium. When we got outside the hospital you could hear the booming of the public address announcer's voice and sometimes the band playing, and we'd make our way across Montlake and over to the stadium. It was crowded, just real crowded and it would start to get kind of exciting then, and I'd pretty much follow Dad cutting across the flow to the faculty gate and that's when he'd give me my ticket and then we'd go through. Back then, even if it wasn't a big game and we were just playing Cal or the Ducks or someone, it still felt good to get to go and have a reserved seat and just to be there.

"Okay, how we doing?"

Dad would usually check on me after we got through the gate and were about to go up the big spiral ramp to the upper deck.

"Okay."

And then we'd head up the ramp and it was a long haul especially if you weren't in that good of shape like me or Dad, but up on top you could see out over the lake and across to Bellevue and the wet houses and trees covering the hills and along the shoreline and the clouds right above the hills.

I liked those days at the games and being glad that you lived in Seattle and feeling like it was your town and that you belonged there and sitting with Dad and feeling like everything was all right.

So we'd go through the tunnel into the stands in the upper deck and boy were we up high looking down over the field and the teams warming up on the grass and the rest of the stadium filling up below us and in the distance, beyond the stadium across the field, the cemetery on the long, low-rising hill and the traffic on thirty-fifth avenue beyond the cemetery and on the other side the houses of Ravenna.

And usually it was cold up there and so steep and crowded that we all felt like some kind of big crazy family who were all just a little nuts for coming way up into the upper deck and squeezing into the jammed narrow benches in the wind and cold to watch the Huskies on a Saturday afternoon.

And it seemed back then like each game was going to be the one when we'd finally start winning and become an important team and that at the kickoff everyone would be very excited and cheering loudly and even after the other team got ahead everyone still thought we'd win until there were only a few minutes left in the game and we knew we wouldn't.

"How about a hot dog? Will you go get them?"

Dad would usually get his wallet out just before the half when people would start heading down for the tunnels and put some dollars in my hand and then I'd head down alone unless he had to use the men's room and then we'd make our way down together.

It was real crowded on the ramp behind the deck where the refreshment stands were, but still up high and with a good view south of the lake and the floating bridges crossing the lake and the tree-covered back side of Capitol Hill rising up gradually from the lake shore.

"My, oh, my."

Dad would usually give a sigh after we got our hotdogs that said it looks like we're going to lose again, because even though we might not be that far behind at the half you could just tell, and Dad seemed to know first.

Once we had a quarterback who was famous and everyone in America knew him and everyone knew the Huskies. His name was Sonny Sixkiller and he was an Indian and his number was six and when he'd score a touchdown it would be good for six points and everyone would yell, *six! six!* He was on the cover of all the big magazines and he looked like an Indian with black hair and kind of brown skin and an Indian face. Maybe he was from one of the tribes around here, but I don't know which one. Maybe the Sammamish. I don't know. Or maybe the Stilliguamish. Sometimes my pals and I would pretend they were actually the Guamish who were just reaffirming their name: *You a Guamish? Stilligumaish. Still? Still.* I guess we weren't very sensitive.

Sonny Sixkiller, *six!, six!*

With Sonny, though, we always won more games than we lost, which for the Huskies was an accomplishment. But still, six and five. Big deal.

Sonny sure could throw that ball, though. He could throw it the length of the field. He could throw it out into Lake Washington if he wanted to. *Coach, where are all the balls? Try Kirkland.* Nah, I'm kidding. I wonder if Sonny ever had six carries for six yards? That'd be about right for a quarterback. It'd probably give the sports announcers a sore jaw, too. *Number six, Six, six for six yards.*

Sonny Sixkiller, *six!, six!*

So anyway, Dad and I would make our way back up to our seats and watch the second half and stomp our feet in the cold and maybe get excited a few times, but usually the excitement wouldn't last and then we'd start thinking about other things.

"Are you coming over for dinner tomorrow? Your mother's making pot roast."

"I don't know."

"We'd like it if you did."

"I'll let you know tomorrow."

Later in the car on the way back through the city as it rained and the clouds and dark came down low, I'd start to think about things as Dad drove through the heavy traffic on the wet streets, playing the radio real loud because he couldn't hear that well, listening to the other scores and statistics to the game.

Maybe I should take more classes at school, I would think, looking out through the wet windscreen as the wipers flicked back and forth. I can't keep packing furniture forever. Maybe I should move, go south, live somewhere else for a while.

But it was hard to think too much because the radio was so loud and the traffic so thick with all the streets leading away from the stadium jammed with cars, and policemen at every intersection directing the flow. But after a while we'd break out of the game traffic and get on a good street and be cruising along for my place.

"Let us know, Mitch."

"Okay."

So even if there was a lot to think about it was still good to have gone to the game and watched the Huskies play, even if they lost, and to have been with Dad for a while, because sometimes just forgetting about things was the best thing to do, and that's what a Saturday afternoon Husky game could do.

TINY'S

"Can we stop soon?"

"You need to go again?"

"Yes," she said, and looked out the passenger window to the low mountains and hills passing beyond the road.

"There's a town a few miles up. Can you wait until then?"

"Yes, I think so." She had been waiting for most of the past year. Waiting for them to decide how best to fight the tumors. They had already taken one eye and were threatening the other. The doctors had never seen anything like it, they had said. They had never seen them come to the surface like this.

Frank, squinting, shifted in the driver's seat, his hand at the top of the wheel. He glanced over at her left profile, as striking as ever, even in her fifties with the stunning beauty of her youth now a blurred reflection, like through ripples in a pond.

She turned and looked at him and the bulges came into view.

"What?" she said, knowing what.

"Nothing," he said. "Are you sure you can wait?"

"Maybe we better pull over," and she turned back.

A wide spot on the dirt shoulder appeared, and, slowing, he pulled off the road. A truck approached from the other direction and she waited until it passed before opening the door. Traffic on the old state highway was light, most was on the interstate where they would be in an hour. Now, on the October Monday-morning, there was almost none.

Frank got out, too, and walked around to the front of the car, and, slowly, leaned against the hood. He felt the hot metal and stood and began strolling up the shoulder. Off the road were some trees where Sharon could relieve herself and she started for them. The Montana sky was bright and the wind blew lightly down from the hills and across the scrub. Frank, strolling, kicked at the dirt and the dust blew away and he looked at the distant mountains, now yellow and gold, turning with the color of fall. There would soon be snow at the tops.

"Frank…" Sharon was buttoning her pants near the trees, looking at the ground. "Take a look at this"

Turning, he could see the bulges even from a distance, the dark areas; and his expression instinctively turned to the neutral guarded look one takes when randomly encountering the physical misfortunes of strangers: no shock or pity, and no excessive friendliness, which could be even more offensive. A simple, alert, expression of pleasant neutrality. Except that she was not a stranger. She was his wife, his second wife, the beauty and spirit he had been seeking for what seemed too much of his adult life. Her spirit, though, if anything, had grown since the diagnosis; and he strolled over to where she stood.

"Look at this." She was staring at the ground, to an old sign, broken and faded, lying in the dirt: *Tiny's, Cashmere*. "Didn't we pass there on the way to your mother's last year? On the way to Seattle?" The muscles of her face attempted to smile, but since the last surgery were not capable of the movement. She looked at him with the full of her face—the straight auburn hair parted in the middle, screening off the sides—with the dark and scarred bulges that leaped from the right half, with the eye that was no longer there and the smile that was only a memory.

Frank squatted in front of the sign, only a foot high, maybe two wide, like some kind of for-sale sign one would stick in their front yard. He picked it up and turned it over, which was blank. "Son of gun, Sharon...yes, just before Leavenworth. You're right. Son of a gun...Tiny's."

"How much farther, Mommy? Are we there yet?"

"Be quiet, Frankie. I'm trying to read."

The signs had been increasing as they drew nearer, appearing every few miles or so, even before the pass.

"There's one!" Frankie, in the back seat with Beth, his younger sister, watched wide-eyed as the small sign, barely visible above the clump of brown grass, passed out the car window. Grinning, he turned back to the panel in the comic book he held in his lap. Beside him, Beth continued her quiet conversation with the auburn-haired doll she held, discussing, in serious but friendly tones, what should be done about the shiny hair.

In the comic, Batman was in serious trouble, but Batman was always in serious trouble, but not really because

Batman's troubles were always being instigated by fools, or buffoons, or blatant evil. And Batman, whose face was chiseled strong and handsome, was not going to stay in trouble for long from fools or buffoons who looked like fools or buffoons.

"See the one up on the rock, Frankie?" Ed, Frankie's father, nodded to where low cliffs of basalt rose as the road passed into a narrow canyon. Someone had climbed part of the cliff to place a sign on a small ledge, the smooth dark rock rising behind, accenting the small white sign: *Tiny's, Cashmere.*

"Wow!" Frankie said from the backseat, grinning widely as he looked at the cliff. "How did they get *that* one there? Did someone climb up there, Daddy?"

"Someone must have, son."

Frankie turned completely around to watch the sign out the back window for as long as he could, even after it had disappeared around the slow-curving canyon wall, straining to see it for longer, trying for a moment, to see it through the rock, like Superman could.

Frankie turned back in his seat and looked again at the comic. He turned the page and began to read the first panel, but his eyes grew heavy and then began to close. He tried to blink them open, but they closed for good and he slumped against the door. Beside him, leaning against the other door, the doll sideways in her lap and wide-eyed toward the window, his sister also slept, as the car continued through the narrow canyon.

There were flashes of light in something like the blackness of outer space, and difficult-to-decipher voices coming from large figures that periodically appeared. The figures were talking to him and sometimes to each other, but he could not quite make out the words, which were distorted, and echoed. He was afraid, but not really, but maybe a little, because bad things didn't really happen to him because his parents protected him from bad things, but he had heard about them and was afraid of them.

The figures became larger and were alive and had bodies and faces but not really but sort of and he woke up with the thudding of the road passing under the tires and the loud hum of the motor as they continued down the highway.

Frankie picked Batman up from the floor and stretched and looked out to the passing rows of apple trees spread below the barren hills and saw the low white buildings approaching up the highway. The car slowed and his mother woke his sister, and Frankie yawned and squinted as they came to the buildings and the dirt parking lot and the tall sign on top of one of the buildings that said *Tiny's* and the large painted letters covering the wall of another building of the same sign.

There were acres of stacked wooden crates for transporting fruit and train tracks that ran close behind the buildings. The summers were hot in this part of the state and the low buildings, where the fruit was stored, were painted white to reflect the burning sun.

Ed parked the car in the dusty lot where people were returning from the tent-covered stand with bags of fruit and small boxes of candy, and others stood about or walked toward the tent or the lunch counter that was in one of the buildings.

"Time for lunch," Frankie's mother said, and they got out of the car and crossed the dirt lot toward the sprawling market.

"Do we get hamburgers, Mommy?" Beth asked, still carrying the doll.

"If you'd like, honey, or sandwiches."

"Will Tiny make the hamburgers, Daddy?" Frankie asked, walking beside his mother and father and little sister. "Why is he called 'Tiny', Daddy? You said he was big."

"That's what someone told me, son. I don't know, maybe the name is supposed to be funny."

Frankie, smiling, walking with his family, thought about this for a moment, deciding, yeah, it would be funny, if he really was big. It would be funny because his name is Tiny; and he smiled very widely because it was funny.

"I'm hungry," said Ed. "Let's eat."

They walked through the open-walled tent, the ground covered in wood chips, tables stretching in each direction with bins of fruit, people picking out the fruit and filling bags.

They came to the lunch counter where the tent connected to one of the buildings and sat at the last empty booth. Through an opening behind the counter they could see into part of the kitchen where several cooks in white aprons and cloth hats were frying hamburgers and preparing sandwiches.

"Is Tiny back there, Daddy? Will we see him?" Frankie, from the booth, strained to see through the opening beyond the counter. The men, only their heads and shoulders visible, prepared the lunches.

"I don't know, son."

Frankie smiled again: *Tiny*, he thought, but all he could imagine was a short man. "Mommy, I have to go to the bathroom," Frankie said.

"Okay, dear. Do you have to go, Beth?"

Beth shook her head, no.

"Are you sure, sweetie?"

Clutching the doll, she shook her head again.

"Ed, do you want to go with Frankie?"

"Let's go, Franklin, your mother will order the hamburgers for us."

They slid out of the booth and walked back to the tent where the sign for the restrooms had been. It pointed to an area at the back where the tent connected to the lunch building, and, walking on the wood chips, they started for it. When they got to the back they saw the sign again, pointing down a dim hallway of the lunch building. In the tent, the open walls had let in everywhere the bright light of the warm August day.

"Heck," Ed now said. "Frankie, you go use the restroom, I think I left my wallet in the car."

"Okay," Frankie said; and his father turned and headed back into the tent.

The hallway, narrow and dim and enclosed by white plywood, had a light bulb hanging from the low ceiling, with daylight from the open-tent walls too far away. A woman with her small daughter emerged from the end of the hallway and passed by. There was a barely open door that led into the back of the lunchroom and Frankie, continuing down the hallway, looked in. He saw some stacks of boxes and heard some voices but couldn't see any people. He went further down the hall and saw the men's sign just as a man came out. Pushing the door open and going in, he was enveloped by the stench of urine and mold; and he went quickly to the tall, porcelain urinal. To the side, a man with a hat washed his hands at the sink. In the stain-covered mirror, Frankie could see the man's unshaven face and what looked like a bulbous, pock-marked nose. Frankie carefully peed into the urinal, the floor smelly and sticky, as the man, not looking in the mirror, took a paper towel, dried his hands, and left. Another man came in with his son, the boy younger than Frankie, and Frankie finished peeing.

"Right here." The man guided his son to the other urinal, as Frankie, zipping his pants, went to the sink. He carefully washed his hands and looked in the dirty mirror, but his reflection was streaked and blurry, and not how he thought he really looked. But he could still make out his face, and his hair, and he thought that his chin looked a little like Batman's, or someday would, but the rest of his face he didn't know, because Batman wore a mask. So did Zorro and so did the Lone Ranger and so did Frankie, sometimes, when he made one out of black cloth and cut out the eye-holes and played them at home.

He turned his head to see his profile, but the mirror was too dirty and the moldy smell of the room made him want to leave. He took a paper towel and dried his hands and was going to throw it in the waste basket but saw that it was full; damp, wadded, paper towels surrounding it on the floor. He carefully placed the towel on the pile but it rolled off. He picked it up and tried again and again it rolled off. Now he picked it up and pushed down onto the pile, the pile slowly compressing, then carefully releasing, and the towel slowly rising. But it stayed and

Frankie now wanted to leave. He saw the towel out of the corner of his eye as he opened the door and it was still on the pile and he went quickly out the door. Now another man was coming down the narrow hall and he looked at Frankie. The man stopped at the door that had been partially open and opened it wider.

"I'm going home, Lou. Don's coming in. He'll be here within the hour."

A soft voice came from within the room but Frankie couldn't hear the words.

"I said Don's coming in," the man now said very loudly. Then he said: "Get up, Tiny," and he shook his head and continued down the hall to the men's room, walking swiftly past Frankie.

Now Frankie took a step up the hall toward the door, which the man had left open. He moved slowly toward

the door in the dimly-lit hall and could see more of the boxes that he had seen before. He came to the door and looked in and saw a man in a soiled apron attempting to rise from a wood bench, a man whose balance was in great jeopardy as the fatness of his body spilled outward in dimensions not previously fathomable to Frankie. A mass of flesh pushing the pants and shirt—which could not have been commercially purchased—into a space where the bodies of four men should have been. Frozen, Frankie watched the grotesque creature, with enormous effort and strain, rise to its feet, clothes soiled, shoes untied, still bent forward, now straightening, whom, were the computations of weight and mass understood by the boy, which they were not yet, he would have known would have exceeded five-hundred pounds; and the man, finally upright, his breathing labored, looked at the boy, and Frankie turned and walked quickly down the hall.

"Where's Frankie, Ed?"

"He isn't back yet? I left my wallet…"

"Here he comes."

They saw him walking amongst the tables of fruit and the people, and their expressions quickly darkened as they saw the look on the little boy's face, their son.

"What's wrong, Frankie? Did something happen? What is it, honey?"

"Nothing," he said, and felt a growing weight he had not felt before. A weight he knew would be of concern to even Batman and Superman.

"What?" his mother said once more, just as a waitress came up with the hamburgers.

"Anything else?" the waitress asked.

79

"…This is good," said the mother, still looking across the table to where her son sat; and they began to eat the food, except for Frankie, who said he didn't feel well.

"What's Tiny's, Frank?" Sharon asked at the side of the Montana road, standing above the sign in the cool autumn air.

"Oh…it was a fruit stand. They had these signs all over the state. You'd see them sometimes…in far off places. I guess even Montana."

"Was it small?"

Frank looked at Sharon's face, then looked away.

"What?"

"Nothing."

She took a step toward the car. "I'm hungry, Frank, do you want to get something to eat?"

"No, not really."

SEA-TAC

"Next...step through...face the wall...raise hands. Anything in your pockets? Keys? Change? Step over there, please."

"Here?" said Kevin Donald, and he slid in stocking feet across the linoleum to where a large woman directed his feet and arms apart and ran a small baton around the outline of his body.

She gestured toward the exit belt where his laptop and shoes and coat and travel bag sat in gray trays that were stacking up at the end of the belt, and retrieved his possessions. He carried everything over to a bench and sat and put his loafers back on and his laptop back into its case and slipped his belt back through the loops of his slacks.

A middle-aged woman in gray pants and a white sweater walked up and held out her hand. "Kev, I'm going to get a magazine. Let's use your card." Kevin fumbled in a pocket for his wallet and handed Linda, his wife, his *Visa* card, which she took and rolled off with her carry-on bag for the newsstand.

The terminal was crowded and everywhere around him people reassembled the belongings they had removed for security. Shoes were put back on, money, keys, phones returned to pockets, computers placed back in there bags. And then they were off to the gates.

"Jesus," a man said who had sat next to Kevin to tie his shoes. He was somewhat disheveled, heavy, unfashionably dressed, balding. Now he spoke directly to Kevin: "I just lost a two dollar bottle of water. They took me into another room, for Christ's sake. I don't think an ant could get past there. Jesus."

"Yeah, probably not," said Kevin, but the man seemed not to hear, or pay attention, looking off into the crowd as he tied his shoes, preparing for the next leg of his journey.

Pulling his travel-bag and carrying his coat, Kevin walked down the concourse toward the news store, saw Linda coming out, a magazine under her arm.

She came up. "What is it again, C-Gate?…C-Gate." She squinted at her boarding pass, tucked the large glossy further, the handle of her carry-on in her other hand.

"We still have an hour," said Kevin. "Let's find coffee."

"Good, it's good we got through quick," said Linda. "You never know with security."

Everywhere people stood in lines, sat on benches, walked in every possible direction.

Kevin gazed absently through the crowd. "No, you never know. Took me an hour last time I went through. Some kind of high-alert, or something." He looked again at his watch. "Good, let's get coffee."

"There's places at the gate," said Linda.

Above them was a sign pointing to C-Gate. Kevin couldn't remember how long he had been coming to C-

Gate—or B-gate or D-Gate—but it seemed like as far back as he could remember. It seemed like a very long time.

Kevin Donald, standing in the dirt clearing below the Sea-Tac runway, did not know if he could wait for Jenny Phelps' party on Friday night. He was in love with Trudy Barlowitz and it would not be until Jenny's party that he would be able to see Trudy again. She went to Nathan Hale High School. Kevin went to Shorecrest. She had forcefully instructed Kevin not to call; recent parental phone groundings regarding boys, she had explained, her tone succeeding with its apparent intent of frightening Kevin. But, she was also worried about *'Tom,'* she had immediately added—her tone now very feminine, apologetic, conveying deep concern, sounding, Kevin imagined, like love—whom she had *'just broken up with,'* whom, she was worried *'might get upset,'* if he saw her with someone else.

A few feet away, leaning against Doug McBride's Chevy Impala and sharing a joint, Doug and Carl Haskins looked up at the low clouds of the night sky.

"How long is this going to take?" Carl asked, inhaling on the burning joint, one hand shoved into the pocket of his jeans, a light breeze at times blowing back the tails of his unbuttoned flannel shirt, under which he wore a white tee-shirt.

"No idea," Doug said as he scanned the sky. He tapped Carl's arm to indicate it was his turn for the joint. "There were, like, two in a row the last time. It was fucking incredible. Like dropping acid." He took the joint from Carl, his gaze remaining on the sky.

"I don't know," said Carl. "Sunday night. Maybe they don't fly on Sundays."

"Of course they fly on Sundays. If someone's going to Japan, or somewhere, it wouldn't even be Sunday. It'd be Monday…or Saturday…"

Behind the car against which the two high-school seniors leaned, the steep bank of dirt rose up to the edge of the runway, a wide row of green lights extending across the top of the bank. In front of them, marking the flight path, elevated banks of red lights rose at intervals above the dark field that stretched into the distance.

"*Kevin…*" Doug called to Kevin who remained a few feet away. "What's up, man? I haven't heard three words all night."

"Kevin got a heavy arrow from cupid," Carl said, trying not to grin, but did.

"*No shit?*" said Doug. "Who's the lucky lady?"

"Some Hale chick," Carl said.

"—We just met," said Kevin, who also scanned the sky.

"*No, shit,*" said Carl. "We had to wait half an hour for them to finish in the backseat Friday night. Car was shakin'"

"Bull-*shit,*" said Kevin, and turned red, but because of the dark and his long hair, no one could tell. He had tried, but her tickling skills were extraordinary; his hands withdrawing as reflexively as a firm tap under a kneecap.

"*Look*—here comes a plane!" Doug suddenly yelled.

Visible in the distance, coming low through the clouds, the beams of twin lights floated slowly toward them. The low rush of traffic on the nearby highways gradually re-placed by the high whine of the approaching jet engines.

"Get ready! Get ready!" Doug yelled, and Kevin ran over to where Carl and Doug already leaned against the car and leaned back beside them as they faced the approaching aircraft.

"Holy-fuck!" yelled Carl, *"I hope he don't come down short!"*

But the roar of the engines, as the approaching lights grew larger, drowned out the last of Carl's words, even to ears only a few feet away.

Now the lights on the wings were visible extending out from the round nose and the landing gear below the wings; and the high whine of the engines grew deafening, piercing through the even louder low-roar of the exhaust.

Leaning back against the car with pounding hearts, they watched the approaching aircraft pointed at Doug McBride's Chevy Impala expand in size, like an inflating balloon, until it seemed to blank out the entire sky, then passed what seemed just feet overhead; rows of rivets and obscure numbers across the gray metal panels briefly imprinting to their vision before their eyes squeezed shut; and Kevin Donald saw the wide seductive grin of Trudy Barlowitz in the recesses of his mind.

"Double-tall, low-fat, sucree-latte… Linda?"

"Double-Verde Americano, no cream."

Kevin Donald handed his credit card to the smiling dark-skinned clerk behind the counter. She swiped; he signed. Kevin and Linda then joined the crowd waiting for their drinks.

On the wall above them, a sign read: *See something suspicious? Call...* There was a phone number for airport security.

"Holy-fuck... Holy-fuck... Holy-fuck..." Doug Mc-Bride sprinted in tight circles around the dirt clearing in front of the Impala, holding his head between his hands, as the ringing in everyone's ears slowly resided.

Carl slid toward the front of the car and sprawled face up across the hood, his arms extended beyond his head, the joint still burning in his lips. Kevin remained frozen where he had been leaning against the car, head tilted back, eyes still squeezed shut, hands buried in front pockets.

"Holy-fuck... Holy-fuck... Holy-fuck..." Doug continued to sprint around the dirt, then ran to Carl sprawled across the hood, grabbed the joint from his mouth, and resumed sprinting as he toked away.

"Wow," Kevin slowly said, finally opening his eyes. *"That* was un-*real."* He shook his head and blinked several times; he leaned away from the car, momentarily swaying.

"Totally, fucking, unreal," said Carl on the hood, staring into the dark clouds. He called to Doug for the joint, who finally stopped running, and, breathing deeply, brought the last of it over to Carl who held out his hand as he continued to gaze at the clouds.

"How'd you find this place?" Kevin said, coming over to where Doug now stood bent over with hands on knees, inhaling and exhaling deeply, attempting to replenish the oxygen supply he was currently extremely short of.

"...*Chuck*..." Doug managed to wheeze out between the deep breaths. "...*Chuck showed me*..." And then he suddenly stood and in a normal voice inquired with Carl if there was any of the joint left to which Carl held out a tiny glow of red on a tiny piece of white paper that immediately went out.

"Well?" said Kevin, looking off into the distance for more planes.

"Well what?" said Doug, also scanning the sky.

"Well now what?"

"Well now what, what?"

"—Hey. Let's go in the terminal," said Carl.

"And do what?" said Doug.

"I don't know—look at some planes."

"Might as well," said Kevin. "We came all the way down here."

Doug McBride, staring into the night sky beyond the approach-lights, shrugged his shoulders and went to the driver's door of the Impala. Carl got in the front seat, Kevin climbed into the back, and Doug, behind the wheel, revved the engine and pulled out bouncing across the dirt field.

"No, Cindy, I don't know where it is...here's your mother." Kevin Donald, sitting in the crowd below the tall airport windows of Gate C-9, handed his cell phone to Linda, who sat beside him thumbing through her magazine, sipping her coffee. "Cindy wants to know where Boris's other collar is…I don't know, do you?"

"What, dear? Did you look downstairs? In the tool drawer? Go look." Linda tilted the end of the phone away from her jaw. "You told the Hanson's we were going to be away, didn't you?"

Kevin, reading the morning newspaper and drinking his coffee beside Linda, lowered the paper. He looked above the lenses of his reading glasses. "I told Ted twice. I told him a month ago and then I told him again last weekend. He knows."

Linda quickly swung the phone back. "Got it? … Right. And don't forget the theater tickets…as soon as they come, mail them in. All right, dear. Okay. Okay. We'll see you in a few weeks…I love you too. Bye." Linda folded the phone and handed it back to Kevin. She took another drink of her coffee and glanced around the concourse, then went back to the magazine.

Kevin looked out at the continuous movement of people. He glanced at his watch and looked again through his glasses at the newspaper.

Two signs on a wide support pole in front of them said: *No Smoking*, and, *See Something Suspicious? Call…*

Doug McBride, Carl Haskins, and Kevin Donald walked slowly down the wide empty terminal that seemed to stretch on forever. There had been a few people—airline employees, a few travelers—back at the main entrance and check-in counters, but now as they continued out the arm of the concourse there were none.

They came to a soda dispenser and Doug drifted over and stuck a finger in the coin return and pushed a few buttons and moved on.

Out the concourse windows was the black of the runway with the occasional glow of lights on the edges or on a sign or the side of a building.

A janitor slowly mopped the floor in front of a closed door, then continued back toward the main terminal.

Doug pulled a stick of gum from his pocket. He pulled off the wrappers and dropped them on the floor near the wall. He stuck the stick in his mouth. Chewed.

"Look…a jet…" Kevin drifted over to the wall of windows on one side and pressed his face against the glass. Toward the end of the concourse, facing the terminal in a glow of lights, a 707 sat at a gate, its sleek silver cylinder seemingly in a state of suspended animation, before it would be brought back to life and scream hurtling down the runway and into the sky.

Kevin pulled his face away and they continued down the concourse. Above him on the wall was the large letter C.

"Cool," said Carl Haskins when he was down at the gate where the jet was parked, his face against the window, a hand above his eyes to lessen the glare.

Doug and Kevin joined him at the window, directly in front of the nose, the jet aglow with the lights of the runway and concourse, the lights of the cockpit visible through the slanting windows, the cockpit door open and lights extending into the interior. The wings, like thin blades, extended out from the body; the large tires of the landing gear rested on the pavement below.

"Hey…look…" Doug walked over to the empty passenger-holding area that was surrounded by a waist-high barrier. There was a moveable counter in the holding area and beside the counter an open door which led down the loading tunnel to the plane. Beside the door was a sign: *No Admittance.*

Doug leaned against the small gate of the holding area, tried to open the handle but it was locked. He looked again down the lighted tunnel. "Check this out," Doug said as Kevin and Carl came over. He rattled the locked gate once more, looked back down the empty concourse—which led to another concourse which led back to the main terminal—and swung his legs over the waist-high wall.

"Cool," said Carl, and he and Kevin both swung over and followed Doug McBride as he entered the loading tunnel that led to the jet.

Except for Carl, who had once been up in a cousin's four-seat Piper who was a crop duster in the Yakima Valley, none of them had ever been in an airplane before. They had all imagined flying in a plane someday, but in the winter of 1969, seniors in high school in the small northwest city of Seattle, they had never thought once about taking a trip somewhere where you would have to fly on a jet.

They took trips all the time; it seemed like every weekend they got into someone's car and drove to Lake Chelan or Ocean Shores, or maybe Mt. Rainier or Vancouver. Where else would anyone ever want to go? Hawaii?

Maybe. But with the places they went they knew exactly where to stay, where to eat, and where to get enough beer and dope to last for however far or long they were planning on going.

Except for Kevin's father, who had flown a few times to California for business, they didn't know anyone who had ever taken a commercial aircraft anywhere.

Doug turned the corner of the ramp first and entered the open door of the Boeing 707, stepping—like one giant leap for mankind—over the sliver of light between the ramp and the fuselage that revealed the distant pavement below. He stood in the small entry-space for a moment, still chewing gum, and looked at everything and at nothing. Carl and Kevin now came through the door and Doug moved into the lighted cabin, the rows of seats extending to the back of the plane.

"I wonder where it's going?" Carl said.

Doug shrugged and squeezed back past Kevin and Carl and ducked into the cockpit. He stood for a moment, bent over between the two seats, and could see through the windscreen back into the terminal where they had just been. He still didn't see anyone in the terminal.

Now Carl bent into the cockpit behind Doug. There were lights and gages and levers everywhere. Doug tried to sit in one of the seats but couldn't get his body turned right. He pushed on the large lever between the seats but it didn't move.

"I think this one makes it go up and down." He pushed harder but it still didn't move. He flipped a small metal switch a couple of times: up, down, up, down.

"I think that was up," Carl said when Doug had moved on to some buttons.

"No it wasn't. It was down."

"No, man, it was up."

Doug rolled his eyes and pressed a few more buttons. "Where's Kevin?"

They turned and looked down the cabin where Kevin was strolling slowly back up the aisle.

"Pretty cool," said Kevin, as Doug and Carl left the cockpit and came into the cabin to look. "Anyone ever been on one of these?"

"Nah," said Doug, and he closed and opened the cabin curtain.

"Not me," said Carl.

Doug closed and opened the curtain a few more times, he seemed to like the sound. He sat in one of the seats, arms on the armrests, opened one of the ashtrays on the end. He stood up. "Hey, what do you say we go find something to eat? I'm starving."

"Yeah. Good idea," said Carl. "Is there a *Dick's* down here?"

Kevin shrugged. "I don't think so." He bent over to look out one of the windows. "But I don't know, maybe."

"Come on," Doug said. "I think there's a *Big Boy* on 99," and he ducked out the plane door and back into the loading tunnel.

With final glances into the cockpit and back down the cabin, Carl and Kevin followed Doug McBride back into the terminal.

"Good morning. We're about to begin early board-ing of United Flight 619 with direct service to London, Heathrow. Wheelchair and other priority boarding please come to the door…"

Kevin Donald stood and took the empty coffee cups and his newspaper over to a row of receptacles and dis-carded them as Linda, rising from the bench of seats, tucked the magazine into a pocket of her carry-on.

Everywhere out the concourse windows the giant, sil-ver bodies of jets were parked at the gates, the accordion loading-tunnels extended out and attached like some kind of artificial erotic pleasure the plane was indulging in before screaming off again into the heavens.

Directly across from Kevin and Linda, people began filing out a door with the strange dazed-but-pleased look that follows a just completed flight at thirty-five- thou-sand-feet in a winged aluminum tube at six-hundred miles an hour. With the exception of those going to connecting flights, what had most likely begun as a pre-dawn drive or shuttle from home or hotel in another state, followed by the synchronized, pre-flight steps at the terminal, lead-ing to the final exiting of the plane into the destination airport, there was now only a ride left of some distance on the very solid ground of God's Earth.

A young college-age couple with backpacks came out grinning and holding hands; and the girl stretched up to the boy's bearded face who turned and kissed her, neither breaking stride or closing their eyes so as to see where they were going.

When they had moved to the middle of the concourse they turned and faced each other with hands held low to the sides and pressed their bodies against one another and resumed the kiss, a kiss, Kevin thought, as cinematic as Hollywood had ever recorded.

"Kev—you ready?" Linda had begun to inch her way with the crowd moving toward the gate but stopped when she realized Kevin was being distracted by something. But she didn't really see the kissing couple, or make the connection that it was they who were distracting him, and she pulled out her boarding pass when she saw Kevin turn to join her.

"You ready?" she said again as he came up.

He nodded and got out his boarding pass and looked back to where the young couple had been, but they were gone.

As Kevin and Linda waited for their boarding-group number to be called, Kevin reflexively read the signs on the pole beside them: *See Something Suspicious? Call...* and: *No Smoking*. From somewhere he briefly imagined another saying: *No Kissing*.

The crowd was loud and the crowd was noisy at the auxiliary gate for the now four-pm charter-flight to London. The tickets had been purchased four months before (the one-pm departure having once already, to no ones great surprise, been pushed back to four) passports, travelers-cheques, and visas acquired long ago, backpacks filled and youthful lives ready to be changed forever.

Nineteen-year-old Kevin Donald stood with twenty-year-old Peter Carmichael beside the Sea-Tac ashtray cylinder and smoked his Winston-filter as Peter smoked his Camel-filter. Other people stood at the same ashtray, or at one of the others in the crowded room, everyone on the charter-flight, most older than Kevin and Peter, in their mid to late twenties with a few professor-types in their forties, everyone to varying degrees connected to the University of Washington, the charter sponsors, people puffing away, clouds of smoke, like smoke signals, rising everywhere.

If there were ever a time for the calming effects of one's nicotine habit, it was now, before boarding a jet-airplane (most, including Kevin and Peter, for the first time) and flying in the skinny tube all night in the upper atmosphere somewhere over the Arctic Circle (with one fuel stop in Iceland) for jolly, swinging London.

Everywhere people puffed away.

"They don't have parachutes do they?" Peter asked, taking a deep drag and flicking the ash, which, because of his continuous flicking from the moment the cigarette was lit, never acquired any ash that amounted to anything.

"Parachutes?" said Kevin. "I don't think so."

"Let me ask—Tom, there aren't parachutes are there?"

A tall older fellow with a short beard and tweed coat, puffing away as he spoke rapidly to the fellow next to him, turned quickly to Peter and said '*no*' in the middle of his sentence, immediately resuming his dialogue with the other man, repeatedly flicking his ash, finishing the point he had been making. Peter—with whom the man now knew fairly intimately from three hours of cigarettes and random conversations with any and all group members standing nearby as the hyped throng waited to get on the jet—and his question, not seeming particularly unreasonable; unreasonable questions with this group, in this situation, not seeming possible.

"I guess not," Peter said, turning back to Kevin, neither really sure if the question was totally unfounded, neither really caring, but also unable to imagine a scenario on a jetliner where a parachute would work. "Hey...look," Peter nodded toward two girls, sort of flower-child-looking, obviously students, who were laughing and smoking at another ash-can a few feet away. He stubbed out his half a Camel and got out a new one and went over to them.

"Got a light?" The cuter one flicked open a lighter and Peter drew on his Camel. "Where you guys from?"

"Madrona," the girl said. She flicked her cigarette. "Where you guys from?"

"Wedgewood. Where you staying tomorrow?"

This was not a question intended to lead to anything. It was more a question to practice talking to girls, to strangers. A skill they seemed constantly to hear they were supposed to improve. And because everyone in the room was a part of the charter and had had to find a place before hand to stay the first night or two in London, which was a long ways from Seattle, it was the dominant question, and a question Peter could immediately ask this girl with no possible risk of self consciousness. It seemed, in that room, in that atmosphere, had the dominant question been: *do you want to fuck?*, it would have fallen within the same restrictions of emotional-reaction and social-acceptance as: *where you staying tomorrow?*

And depending on one's connections and lodge-finding-skills, of which Kevin and Peter had none previous, the answer to: *where you staying tomorrow?*, which everyone in the room had asked everyone else over the last three hours, ranged from: *I don't know yet,* to, *The High Street Savoy.*

"Kennsington," said the other girl. "What about you guys?"

"Earl's Court," said Peter.

The girls both smiled widely. Peter said thanks and returned to Kevin as the two girls went back to puffing and laughing.

"Where they staying?" Kevin asked.

"Kensington."

"Cool," Kevin said. "Maybe we'll see them."

"...Is it near Earl's Court?" Peter asked.

Kevin shrugged: "I don't know." But the question seemed irrelevant—maybe they'd run into them.

Where you staying?
Are there parachutes?
Do you want to fuck?

Now there was a commotion near the front and Miss Dawson, the charter coordinator, was calling everyone's attention.

"Hello, hello, attention. Everyone. The plane is all set. We've been given clearance to take off. We need the two language groups first, French, German. Everyone else, line up to the left."

The crowd grew louder; coats were put on, documents checked, people moved toward the doors, and then out onto the runway in the bright daylight of the sunny July afternoon.

They walked across the tarmac to where the metal wedge of stairs led to the plane and boarded, flight attendants greeting everyone inside the door and guiding them to their seats.

People began smoking again as soon as the plane was airborne, darkness quickly descending out the windows as they streaked northeast over Canada.

They were served dinner. People read or talked to their seatmate. Soon most lights were out and people went to sleep.

But not everyone.

Kevin Donald didn't go to sleep.

He stayed up all night after dinner and talked to his seatmate who wasn't Peter Carmichael. It was Michelle somebody from Windermere who was also nineteen and flying somewhere for the first time and who also recognized the great social classroom she had accidentally been thrust into where she could practice talking to boys.

Across the aisle a man slept in the first seat, a woman read by the window.

"I think we won't be going to Carnaby Street until Wednesday," Kevin said very self assuredly as he puffed on his Winston-filter. "Another?" He tipped his pack to Michelle who smiled and took one. Kevin lit it. "But we might go there Tuesday. We definitely want to get some clothes."

"My train's at noon. I don't think I'll get to see London at all. Unless on the way back." Michelle drew on the cigarette. She flicked the ash into the little tray on the armrest. She smiled and blew out the smoke.

"Oh, and Piccadilly," Kevin said. "We want to go there, too."

"What's there?" Michelle asked.

"...I'm not sure. Maybe some pubs."

Michelle smoked some more. She turned slightly and leaned again into Kevin. The seats were very close together and the backs were tall so it seemed like being in a private little living room. They had already kissed a few times earlier, not long after the dinner trays had been carted off and people were turning off lights. Kissing is what you did when you were nineteen, or seventeen or sixteen, and you were seated in a private little living room with someone of the opposite sex. This seemed especially appropriate if you were flying on a jet for the first time, headed for London, with no parents around. At their age, in the summer of 1971, kissing is something everyone did at every opportunity, religiously, the thought of not for any length of time—two days, a week—as dreadful as acne or a bad haircut.

Michelle turned and they kissed again. She was pretty cute. Kevin put his arm around her and she nestled in. They finished their cigarettes and soon fell asleep. They had known each other for about two and a half hours.

The plane landed in Reykjavik, Iceland to refuel. Anyone who wanted (which was most of the plane) could get off, but were warned to bring their coats.

Kevin and Michelle, and Peter, who had been seated next to a male English Professor, stood on the runway beside the plane in the dark and drizzle and smoked cigarettes, as did most everyone else. Peter, shivering violently, hadn't brought his coat, but didn't seem to mind, happy and grinning widely in a short-sleeve shirt, inhaling away and yapping loudly about what he'd learned from the English professor about Newcastle Brown Ale: namely that it was very strong. He talked like he might do nothing more for the next eight weeks but drink Newcastle Brown Ale.

Kevin stood in the cold and wind with his arm around Michelle who seemed appreciative of any increased warmth. Kevin hadn't remembered to introduce her to Peter who seemed not to think anything of it, who seemed to think nothing could possibly be more normal than his pal, Kevin, standing on a dark runway halfway around the world—*Where are we? Iceland? Holy fuck!*—with his arm around a girl he had never seen before.

"Newcastle Brown Ale, man."

They reboarded; the plane took off again. Soon light began to appear to the east.

Inside the plane people began to awaken: arms stretched, voices broke the silence.

Near the front, in row six, seats C and D, Kevin Donald and Michelle Bitmore pressed their lips together, heads slowly moving, hands touching cheeks, words whispered into ears.

Out the windows the sun rose on the new day.

Kevin and Michelle stopped for a moment for air and from her shoulder Kevin pulled her hair back to see out the window across the aisle. But the man in the first seat was crouching forward, adjusting his shoes and unknowingly blocking the view. The man turned toward the aisle and saw Kevin gazing through the girl's hair from her shoulder and immediately leaned back to reveal the window. He nodded and Kevin nodded and the plane began its descent down to Europe.

"You excited?" Linda asked Kevin as they settled into their seats on the runway at Sea-Tac, the aisle crowded with people stuffing items into the overhead bins. "You haven't been to Britain since you were a kid, right? How old?"

"Nineteen," Kevin said.

"Wow. That's almost forty years. Well, we'll have to make up for all of that." She leaned into Kevin with a smile for a kiss.

Kevin smiled and leaned over but her cell phone suddenly went off and she leaned back to find it in her bag.

Kevin sat motionless for a moment then slowly leaned back in his seat. He tightened his seat belt and looked out the window. He thought it looked like it might rain but couldn't tell for sure. He turned back and Linda was reading her magazine. He pulled out the airline magazine from the seat pocket and glanced at the articles listed on the cover. He stopped and stared for a moment at the one listed for page eighty-three. He put the magazine back in the pocket and looked again out the window.

'London,' it had said. *'More Swinging Than Ever.'*

ALI CAN'T DRIVE THE BUBBLEATOR TODAY

In the summer of 1969, the weed supply in Seattle mysteriously dried up. It seemed mysterious because although it had always ebbed and flowed, it had never come to a complete end, as everyone in the supply chain knew it had.

Back then, 98% of it came from Mexico and there were various rumors drifting around about chemically contaminated crops and stronger border measures. Sure, there were a few fringe dealers who had leftover, untraditional supply routes—Thai sticks anyone?—but with the city-wide extent of the drought, they weren't parting with anything except over their dead bodies.

> *"Come on, Dawson, I know you got a couple of joints in your house somewhere."*
> *"I wish, man. I wish."*

After it became apparent how extensive the drought was—after the oregano and the left over bags of seeds and stems that scorched everyone's throat had come out—

people slowly came to the realization that they would no longer be able to get stoned: while being good; while being able; or, while in the road.

"Hey, you know if Clark's car is any good?"
"No. Why?"
"He's talking about driving to Nebraska. He thinks weed grows wild there."

People who had not gone for more than a day or two without a hit over the previous few years, were now experiencing life straight for weeks and months at a time.

"I don't know, 'Disraeli Gears' just doesn't sound the same."
"Try 'Ina Godda Divida'."

But while the weed supply came to an end, a potent form of acid which had first appeared the previous winter was still readily available. It was called Orange Sunshine and was to earlier batches—Blue Cheer; Purple-Double-Dome—what hundred-proof Scotch Whisky was to beer. With Orange Sunshine, the world did not faintly resemble the interior artwork of 'Wheels of Fire', it was an exact replica. With Orange Sunshine, your Mother's everyday June kitchen put her most elaborate Christmas living room to shame.

It was early in that same summer of 1969 that, though state employment connections my father was able to secure, I took a job as a busboy in the Food Circus in the old armory building at the Seattle Center. This was the same Food Circus left over from the 1962 Seattle World's Fair, where a dozen or so food vendors ringed the large, open floor, where people sat to eat their food.

We bus boys—were there a few bus girls?—in our neat little uniforms with black bow ties, roamed the floor clearing tables and sweeping, a sort of indoors, county-fair-like atmosphere pervading the cavernous building.

It was here in the Food Circus that the Bubbleator—also left over from the World's Fair (where it had been brought over from the Coliseum for which it had originally been designed)—made its futuristic up and down between the three floors of the Food Circus building.

The Bubbleator was an elevator in the form of a glass bubble, perhaps twenty feet in diameter. The doors opened and people filed in, the operator, who stood at a small metal stand to one side, closed the doors and then pushed either the up button or the down button, depending on which floor the Bubbleator was on. As people sat at tables about the Food Circus floor eating their meals, they could see into the clear bubble of the Bubbleator, filled with people, as it rose up to the balcony or descended to the basement.

The Bubbleator, along with the Space Needle and the Monorail, were the three iconic futuristic-symbols of the twenty-first century, that the 1962 Seattle World's Fair was meant to portray.

Perhaps you are wondering how a weed drought, orange sunshine acid, and the Bubbleator are going to fit together.

Perhaps not.

Let me explain:

Ali was from Palestine. He was in his mid-twenties, an adult, the only adult amongst the mostly high-school-age crew who were that summer's busboys.

Ali was short and with a Mediterranean complexion. His hair was short and very dark and a four-o'clock shadow on his clean shaven face (something we high-schoolers could only dream about) was usually noticeable by noon.

Whereas all the other busboys came from Seattle's outlying residential neighborhoods, Ali lived downtown. He lived, we eventually found out, in an old brick apartment building in what is now called Belltown, with his young wife and their two small children.

In the summer of 1969, no one willingly lived downtown. When everywhere else there were shady lawns surrounding single-family dwellings with an ice-cream truck chiming down the street, who would want to live in the miniature cement-jungle of downtown Seattle?

Perhaps a refugee and his family from Palestine.

As high school kids, most of whom were on their first job, our enthusiasm for spending a sunny summer day inside a 1930's armory building in Seattle's downtown cement-jungle was less than whole-hearted.

Mr. Carlson, would you remind your buddy, Steven, that if he is late one more day, he will be terminated.
Sorry, sir. It's eleven am, he's not used to getting up this early.

Ali's enthusiasm, on the other hand, was limitless. He smiled at everyone. He hurried about, clearing tables the split-second they were vacated. He would get down on all fours on the floor to retrieve a hard-to-get speck of litter from under a table.

On payday, Ali was always the first in line, smiling and laughing and saying *hello hello* to everyone within thirty feet. He would then walk off as swiftly as his short little strides would take him while reading the check he held with both hands in front of his face like a miniature sail.

In the first weeks of June, the first weeks of the job, Brad Harris made what seemed at the time a startling discovery: Ali smoked pot. He didn't smoke it like Brad and all the other Seattle busboys smoked it (or used to, seeing as there wasn't any anymore)—namely, every chance they got—but more as a gesture of social assimilation to his new life in America: occasionally, when circumstance called for it.

"Hashish!" Ali had said that first week while riding in Brad's car, who had offered Ali a ride back to his apartment after work. As soon as they had climbed in, Brad had lit up one of his last remaining joints.

"No, no—not hashish," Brad had laughed, humored, as were all the busboys, when interacting with this strange foreigner and his funny attempts at English. None of them had ever met a non-native-speaker of English before.

"Weed," Brad went on, still laughing behind the wheel. "Pot. Reefer. —Hooligan's Wake."

"Who-la-gun…Wait!" Ali grinned widely.

"Okay," Brad said. "Hashish." And he handed the joint to Ali, who, with a cigarette already burning in one hand, took a deep drag of the pot.

"Hashish, hashish!" Ali now laughed, blowing out the smoke and handing the joint back to Brad.

"Hashish, Ali, hashish," Brad said, also laughing, and he continued driving down the street.

It was an adult woman who operated the Bubbleator. No adult male in the summer of 1969, no matter how hard pressed for employment, was going to dress up in a Star-Trek-like uniform and stand for eight hours at a metal panel in the Bubbleator and press one of four buttons: open; close; up; down.

Most of the days that I worked the operator was Julie: a young though hardened-looking blonde with red lipstick who managed to smile just enough to keep the job; although there were other operators I occasionally saw from time to time. And although we weren't unionized, management adhered to the standard union schedule of a fifteen minute break in the morning and afternoon, and thirty minutes for lunch.

It was then, during the operator breaks, that one of us busboys would take over at the controls of the Bubbleator.

At age sixteen, in sleepy Seattle-town, there are feelings of power and then there are feelings of *POWER*. Operating (or, 'driving', as we used to call it) the Bubbleator for fifteen minutes, definitely fell into the latter.

"Carlson, you're on today to spell Julie at three."
"Yes, sir!"
—Open; close. Up; down—

The euphoria we felt (*Mom, Mom, I got to drive the Bubbleator today!*) as we stood at the raised panel and awaited the crowd to file in—everyone staring at you, as though their lives were in your hands, their thoughts almost telepathic: this thing's just an elevator, isn't it? We aren't *going* anywhere, are we?—was a euphoria we would spend the rest of our lives trying to duplicate.

"Hello, and welcome to the Bubbleator...originally used in the Coliseum during the 1962 Seattle World's Fair...we will now be ascending to the Food Circus balcony..."

"Parker!...did you hear Harris went up twice last week?!... instead of going down to the basement!?"
"No shit?"

"Mr. Fenner says no more Bubbleator for him."
"Holy fuck. How's he taking it?"
"Not good, man, not good."

And so the summer went, strolling the Food Circus floor (watches checked every four minutes) the great sphere of the Bubbleator rising and lowering in the background.

Then came August and for Brad Harris far too many days without a smoke—and we are not referring to Virginia Slims. Even Ali asked from time to time if Brad had anymore 'who-la-gun-wait'.

"Harris, what's this, 'who-la-gun-wait', Ali keeps asking about?"

"Hooligan's Wake. I told him it was another name for weed. I just made it up one day."

"Hooligan's Wake?"

With kids from different parts of the city employed as the Center busboys, different drugs appeared from time to time in the locker room: mostly amphetamines; various psychedelics; occasionally someone trying to pass off a joint of God-knows-what to the very naïve.

Ali tried as best as he could to take it all in, this wealthy, modern land of America, where everything worked and no missiles or bombs dropped from the sky. He wanted to be a part of his new country, and he wanted to be a part of it as quickly as he could.

Unfortunately, with few other Palestinians in town, he was left with his high-school age co-workers as the Americans he was most in contact with, as the unknowing guides to the land and people with whom he and his family now lived.

As his need grew to avert the isolation he must so deeply have felt, a few of the busboys were even invited into his home, Ali eager and accustomed to showing new friends where he lived and introducing his young family.

"Cool rug, Ali…looks old."
"Seventeenth century!"

And so came the week that Orange Sunshine swept into the locker room, its afterglow still radiating on young faces from the previous night's indulgence.

With the initial era of psychedelia winding down—but now well entrenched in the culture—its existence was known to Ali in a way similar to his awareness of the existence and essence of the full blown capitalism he now lived in, or, of Christianity, the country's dominant religion. He knew they affected everyone's life, but could not tell in exactly what way, or how strongly.

Capitalism.

Christianity.

Psychedelia.

And so Brad was stunned, and terrified, when, after asking Ali in the locker room at the beginning of the Wednesday shift if he wanted to buy a hit of the Orange Sunshine he was selling (*you can split it in two, man*), and Ali paid him two dollars (one more than what he was selling it for to everyone else), Ali quickly tossed it into his mouth and swallowed.

"Ali! No! What are you doing?"

"Lucy in sky with diamonds," Ali said laughing as he grabbed a bus tray and headed for the floor.

I found him about two hours later. He was sitting on the floor behind a cabinet down a short hallway that led to an electrical maintenance room, his empty bus tray held sideways under one arm, his white washrag draped over his head like an Arab sheik, staring up at the low ceiling, mouth partially open.

"Ali. Ali. What are you doing?"

After a few moments he slowly turned his head and looked at me, then turned back to the ceiling.

I let Harris and Peterson know where he was right away, but we couldn't let Jenny Stewart see him, the lone girl working that day, who kept asking where Ali was, who would freak out and tell Mr. Fenner that Ali was sitting on the floor staring at the ceiling, or, worse, tell one of the young, uniformed Seattle police cadets who summer-interned as security on the Food Circus floor.

A half hour later Mr. Fenner, with his horn-rimmed glasses and flat-top (this, in August of 1969; recent stories in the papers of some sort of music-festival in upstate New York) made one of his periodic appearances from his back office, stretching his legs, smoking a cigarette, letting his young crew of busboys know that he did exist, that he did have a pulse. He went over to the Orange Julius and got in line.

"Oh, fuck," Brad Harris said to me as we jointly cleared a large group-table across the floor from the Orange Julius.

To one side, the Bubbleator rose up from the basement.

"What are we going to do?" Brad said, his hand sweeping up paper cups and plates in a kind of slow motion. "He finds Ali, Ali might tell him."

"I don't know, idiot. How could you let him take it?"

"He just did—just like that. I thought he knew what it was."

Suddenly, toward the maintenance hall, Ali appeared and streaked across the floor, the wash rag still on his head, moving so fast it seemed almost a run, but it wasn't, just a blur of short rapid strides. He cleared two tables with a sweep of his arm, then suddenly stopped; he adjusted the rag on his head, then took off for the dumpster room down another hall.

Mr. Fenner—his back and skinny shoulders to the floor; the top of his head like a small shelf—inched closer to the Orange Julius counter.

Across the floor, the Bubbleater rose to the balcony; Julie's red lips, framed by long strands of blond hair, seeming to float above the control stand; the opaque form of her figure visible through the clear plastic.

Harris, with a full bus tray, headed for the dumpster room.

I cleared another table and looked up to see Mr. Fenner—a straw between his lips from the large Orange Julius he held, the burning cigarette in his other hand—waving at me to come over. I headed for him across the floor.

At the balcony, the Bubbleator let out a load of passengers.

"Carlson," Mr. Fenner said when we met below the towering Food Circus ceiling, "have you seen Ali?"

"Yeah, I…uh…saw him a while ago."

"Remind him, he's got the Bubbleator at three."

"Oh-*kay*."

Mr. Fenner looked over the floor as he sucked on his Orange Julius. Jenny Stewart cleared a table over by Mr. Lee's Mongolian Steakhouse. Nearby, Adrian Carlyle carried the broom kit: a short broom, and a dust pan at the end of a handle that folded close when you lifted it off the floor. He stopped and flicked a couple of cigarette butts into the pan.

Mr. Fenner took another deep suck from his drink, scanned the floor once more, then headed for his office at the back of the building, the shelf tilting: left, right, left, right

From the balcony, the Bubbleator began its descent.

❦

"Ali, man, you okay?" Brad Harris stood above Ali who sat on the floor between two dumpsters, the rag now tied around his neck like a scarf.

Ali looked at Brad and said something in a foreign language. He looked away and began to sing an American sounding song in the same foreign language.

(Later, Brad Harris swore he was singing 'Jimmy Mack'.)

There was no mistaking it, man. It was Jimmy Mack.

"Ali, you gotta go home," Brad Harris said to Ali who had stopped singing, who remained on the floor between the two dumpsters.

Ali did not look good. He glanced up at Brad, his eyes dilated like a pair of bowling balls.

114

"Ali, you gotta go home," Brad said again. "Come on, man."

Ali looked at his watch. *"Fuck-a-banana!"* he suddenly said, startled. "Almost three o'clock. I got Bubbleator!"

"No, Ali—no, no, no. You gotta go *home*, man. You're going to get into trouble. —The police might come. No Bubbleator."

Ali shot his eyes to Brad when he heard 'police'. He looked away. "...Orange Sunshine..." he said to no one and looked again at the ceiling.

"Here." Brad extended his hand down and helped Ali off the floor. Ali stood for a moment, brushed off his pants, removed the cloth from his neck. From down the hall came the echo of footsteps.

Jenny Stewart appeared with a full bus tray. *"Here* you guys are. You gonna let me do all the work? —Hey, Ali,

Mr. Fenner's looking for you. You're up for the Bubblea-tor." She stopped and looked for a moment at Ali. "…Ali, you okay?"

Ali didn't answer and abruptly headed down the hall.

"What's with him?" Jenny emptied her bus tray into the dumpster.

"He's sick."

"What's wrong with him?"

"I don't know." Brad took a step toward the Food Circus floor. "He's going home. Ali can't drive the Bubblea-tor today."

We finally convinced Ali to leave. Peterson called a taxi and snuck out with him and told the driver where he lived. Peterson had to forcefully pull Ali's bus tray from him as Ali sat in the back, Ali repeating over and over that it wasn't five o'clock yet, when his shift would end.

I had to tell Mr. Fenner that Ali got sick and went home. It happened about twenty minutes after he left.

"Where the hell is Ali?" Mr. Fenner said when he came up suddenly behind me as I cleared a table. "He had the Bubbleator—" Mr. Fenner looked at his watch, "—*ten minutes ago.*"

"He got real sick, sir. He had to go home."

"What? Why didn't he tell me? And where is Peterson? Who's going to give Julie her break? It was supposed to be Ali."

"Sorry, sir. Ali can't drive the Bubbleator today—but I will."

Mr. Fenner abruptly turned and headed off across the floor. From his receding back he jabbed a finger toward the Bubbleator, which had just rose up from the basement. A jab that, had it made contact, would have popped it. Inside, I could see Julie and her red lips, bobbing behind the control panel, searching the Food Circus floor for her replacement.

I stuck my bus tray under a table and headed over.

Harris and Peterson went over to Ali's to check on him later that night, Ali's wife answering the intercom and buzzing them in when they rang. She opened the door to the apartment after they came up, a scarf over her head, dressed in a colorful full-length skirt, a small child on her hip. From somewhere inside they heard Ali call them in.

Ali sat in a large stuffed chair in the small living room, staring at the TV that flickered in the corner. On the floor at his feet, his four-year old son played with a couple of toy trucks. "Come in, come in," Ali said again. He gestured to the couch as his wife closed the door and went to the kitchen, the child on her hip turning wide-eyed to look at the two visitors.

The pungent aroma of simmering spices filled the apartment.

"How you feeling, Ali?" Brad asked as he and Peterson sat on the couch. The curtains were closed and the room was dark but for the TV, and a lamp that glowed on a small table. Several framed plaques of Arabic inscription hung on the walls.

"Good, good," Ali said, sounding tired. "...Not good at work."

"You weren't supposed..." Peterson began to talk but Harris jabbed him to stop.

"Danny told Mr. Fenner you got sick," Brad said. "I think everything is okay."

Ali spoke to his son in foreign words and pushed one of the trucks toward him.

"Mr. Fenner not mad?" Ali asked.

"Nah. I don't think so."

Ali looked at Harris with an expression of weariness. "I didn't know where I was... It was not Seattle...Food Circus..." He looked off for a moment. "...I see Gaza... the hills... I hear planes..."

Harris and Peterson looked at each other. "Don't worry about it, Ali," Harris said. "You'll feel okay tomorrow."

"...U.S...very strange land..." Ali leaned over and turned his son on the floor to reach a truck.

Harris and Peterson looked at each other again. "Okay, Ali," Harris said. "We just wanted to see how you were doing." They moved to the edge of the couch and stood. "Take it easy, Ali. We'll see you in a few days." They went to the door.

"...Very strange land..." Ali said to no one as he moved his son some more and looked again at the TV. A wide-smiling woman in an apron poured laundry from a box into a washer and then held a white blouse up to the camera, showing both sides.

"See you later, Ali," Harris said as Ali continued to watch the TV.

Ali raised a hand but didn't answer and Harris and Peterson went out the door.

FRIDAY NIGHT

It was Friday night and early October, and it was cloudy and dark and had rained lightly that afternoon but it was not raining now. Mark and Steve's apartment, which was actually a unit of an old tri-plex, was in the
north part of the city, which was mostly old residential areas but was not considered out in the suburbs because they were still within the city limits but where the suburbs began was only a few miles more to the north. Mark and Steve had both grown up in the north part of the city and gone to the same high school together but they were now twenty-one and twenty and attended separate community colleges. They knew each other well and mostly knew the same people and it was now Friday night and in the fall they always felt a little older because that was when they usually started new yearly cycles in their lives and since high school the yearly cycles that always seemed to begin in the fall had always made them feel a little older.

But they also were young and on Friday nights it felt good to be young and Mark and Steve had a new apartment and they would soon be doing what felt best and that was going out on Friday night and having a good time.

It was a little awkward living together because it was the first time they had lived with each other, although they had done many things together before, and they had only had the apartment a month and a half and during that first month they had both been gone most of the time on separate end-of-summer trips, and they had not lived out of their parent's homes much before, but mostly they just felt a little awkward with everyone.

But it was Friday night now and all that school business for the week was behind them and they didn't feel awkward now or if they did they didn't care because they felt so good.

Steve sat in the kitchen and smoked a cigarette and talked with different friends on the phone and was very alert because it was Friday night and one of the things he liked best was going out on Friday nights and going to parties and to taverns and seeing his friends and drinking and getting high and being and talking with good-looking girls and Steve looked good and his clothes looked good but they weren't expensive or stylish or over projecting of an image and they felt good to him. And he was alert because he was going through the preliminaries of a good Friday night and who he talked to now and the plans he made now were important to having a good Friday night and he was good at those kinds of plans and he felt good about them.

But Steve also didn't care if there wasn't much going on on a Friday night with the people he knew, because he didn't have to go out and have a wild time every Friday night and he knew that that could get old and that the best Friday nights would be the rare ones when everything just worked out right and he was in the mood for a lot of Friday night things to happen. There had been many Friday nights when the mood and desire were there but the things that make a Friday night good had just not happened.

But tonight couldn't help but be a good one because there was always Hilling's house to go over to if nothing else was going on, and Hilling was a good friend and a lot of fun and he always had special dope to smoke so they could always get good and stoned and then walk over to the *Star* and drink a pitcher of beer and probably see some more people they knew there. And then the thought that someone might get him high on some cocaine went quickly through Steve's mind, but it wasn't an important thought and had just come quickly in the middle of a chain of rapid thoughts and he went on to new thoughts right away; but he knew all about cocaine and had known about it for a long time and what people took it, and he felt that he took care of himself pretty well and was independent, but the thought did cross his mind.

Mark sat in the living room listening to the stereo, thinking about what was going on in his life now, now that he had finally decided to go back to school and really be serious about it. He thought about how it was different now, now that he was doing something that seemed important and respectable, but mostly he just liked school and the people who went to school, and then he thought about the two girls in his sociology class and the girl in his math class and how they had seemed to be like him.

But it was Friday night now and Mark was glad and he felt good just sitting in his own living room on his own furniture in the atmosphere that he and Steve had made, or what they had been forced to make with what few items they had scraped together to furnish the apartment. But it was a good atmosphere and the stereo was good and Mark was glad about that because the music from the records they played was important as a kind of stabilizer for everything and it was good music and they identified strongly to it and to the people who made the music and Mark felt that he and those people and all their friends shared a personal dislike for a lot of things in the world but the music and Mark's listening to it and their all feeling good by it, and their all knowing that there were a lot of screwed up things in the world, made them feel that they were better than those screwed up things and ahead of them, and that made them all feel good.

And it was Friday night and Mark didn't have to do a thing until Monday morning except read some school books which he could do on Sunday night over at his parents, and he sat on the couch and enjoyed the music. He liked that feeling a lot of not having anything he had to do, and on Friday nights in the fall at his age he liked that feeling the most.

Then the phone rang and it was Smith again and he had found out that Lyle and Bret and maybe Scott Klein were going over to a friend of Bret's who knew where a big party in Ballard was and he would call from Bret's when he got there to tell Mark where the party was, and where he'd be for sure later that night, and then he asked to talk to Steve again. And he told Steve that Pete and his girlfriend had said they were going to a party in Laurelhurst and that they'd probably go out to Hilling's and the *Star* later on. Steve had figured that that was probably what Pete was going to do, but he thanked Smith anyway and then hung up the phone and still seemed to be pretty alert.

Then Steve lit another cigarette and walked into the living room and flopped down into the big chair and listened more attentively to the stereo and looked at the painting that was hanging on the wall. And Mark came out of the bathroom and flicked off the light and half-danced to a part of the song that was playing and put on his coat and checked to see if he had rolling papers. And Steve took his coat off the back of the chair that was next to the speaker and put it in his lap and tapped his foot to the music. And Mark turned up that part of the song that they both knew had been coming, and it was pretty loud, and they both really liked that part of the song a lot and it felt good to them. And then the song ended and it was the end of the album and the apartment suddenly seemed to be more empty and they could now faintly hear the sounds of the cars passing down 145th street. But they didn't really think about those sounds from outside that they could now faintly hear, and Mark turned off the stereo and they both turned off some lights and then they walked out the door and into the dark to go have some fun on a Friday night.

A GOOD PLACE TO BE

The truth about it is, though, this: that I like the solitude, the aloneness, that it makes for a kind of feel, a feel deep down inside that you know.

Maybe that's why it can feel kind of good at eight o'clock at night in early May when it is still light and you go for a walk down by the canal, around the pleasant Montlake area, or somewhere near the water. And in the early evening all the young people your age are out and going different places and they are all together and you are alone and it is still daylight and you know it will stay daylight for another hour and you can walk on the path along the canal and there are many boats going through the cut and you wonder who they are to have gotten so much money and you know you will never have it.

But if you keep going in a westerly direction toward Portage Bay you will be facing the most light and you can be on either the hospital side, which means you are at the University—and when is that not a good place to be as long as the students are away?—or on the other side, which means you are in the pleasant residential neighborhood, and that is also a good place. And on that side if you keep walking west along the cut from under the low arching bridge you will come to the wide grassy park with the old thick-trunk trees bordering the bay at the entrance to the cut and then you can take in a lot of Portage Bay and the boat-packed marinas lining the shores and the house-covered hill rising up across the bay. And standing on the grass of the park you are only a foot above the flat, choppy water.

So that is why I sometimes like this going around alone, at that time of year, in the early evening, in that area, because it is easier to think when you are alone, and to dream: and if you keep walking across the park to one of the tree-lined Montlake streets with the old brick houses and the neatly kept yards you can dream about what it would be like to live there, and probably work at the University, but you know you won't ever have the money or chance for that either.

So you climb back into your no-good car, and there is still some evening light, and pick a good driving route along the water and take just that: a good drive back to your house or your shitty little apartment or wherever it is that you live, and stop at a small bar along the way and drink a glass of beer, and still know that you have had a very good evening in Seattle.

DRIVE

The next clear, winter morning, cold-clear—you'll know it's clear because there'll be ice on the windows—get up and into your car and drive down to University Village and up the 45th street viaduct to the U-district, and when you get to the top and you see the Olympic Mountains don't ever forget it.

About the author

Rick Fordyce grew up in north Seattle. He has been published in *Crab Creek Review* and is the author of the novel, *Glen*. He lives in Seattle and Cape Cod.

CPSIA information can be obtained at www.ICGtesting.com
Printed in the USA
BVOW05s0917280414

351834BV00008B/12/P

9 781939 166425